EMMA IN LOVE

Also by Honor Arundel

Emma in Love

HONOR ARUNDEL

THOMAS NELSON INC.

NEW YORK   CAMDEN

No character in this story is intended to represent any actual person; all the incidents of the story are entirely fictional in nature.

Fourth Printing, April 1974

Copyright © 1970, 1972 by Honor Arundel

All rights reserved under International and Pan-American Conventions.
Published by Thomas Nelson Inc., Camden, New Jersey.

Library of Congress Catalog Card Number: 70–180290
International Standard Book Number: 0–8407–6204–6
Manufactured in Great Britain for Thomas Nelson Inc.

I

I walked home wearily through the November dusk. It was my job to do the housekeeping and this meant getting off the bus one stop early and buying food for supper in the little cluster of shops at the corner of Warrender Park Road and Marchmont Road where Richard and I lived. So as well as my school bag—which seemed to get heavier every week—I carried a string bag filled with three pounds of potatoes, a loaf of bread, a hard salad cabbage and half a pound of boiled ham.

A slight drizzle was falling which made the pavements look as though they were sweating and the cars sent up a fine spray of liquid mud. Their lights and the lamp-lights and the lighted shop windows were blurred; the trees, on which only a few ragged leaves still hung, looked haggard and desolate. Edinburgh was not looking its best.

At first Richard had agreed to do his share of the shopping since he often had free time in between lectures but he forgot so often that I had decided it was less trouble to do it myself. It was no fun coming home from school to find that we had run out of bread and that there was nothing in our food cupboard except a tomato or a tin of sardines.

Just before I turned into our road I paused, mentally checking that I had remembered everything because I had no intention of coming out again. I would draw my new orange curtains to shut out the dripping evening, light my gas fire and write my history essay. And if Richard was not playing the piano I would put on my transistor radio which had been a goodbye present from Aunt Patsy and Stephen. Mostly I enjoyed hearing my brother practise but sometimes I liked to hear a completely different sort of music, a proper orchestral concert for instance or pop songs.

I put my key into the lock and tiptoed across the hall hoping that Mrs. Thomson, the landlady, would not hear me. She was a friendly body who often tried to lure me into her kitchen for cups of tea and gossip. Her grey hair was always in rollers and covered with a head scarf and I believed she only took them out when she went to the Bingo on Friday nights and to church on Sundays. She called me 'my lassie', fussed over me when I looked tired, and was always hoping that Richard and I fed properly.

'I know about young folk,' she would say, shaking her head wisely, 'they live on buns and bars of chocolate.' But she was quite wrong. Richard and I, on our narrow budget, ate extremely well and we both preferred things like brown bread, cheese and salad to tins of slimy spaghetti.

Mrs. Thomson lived on the ground floor where she had a front room which she never used, full of family photographs and nicknacks, a bedroom, and a kitchen where she really spent her life. She was always drinking tea or just about to drink tea.

6

Richard and I had a room each on the first floor with a kitchen and a bathroom we shared with two Nigerian medical students who lived on the top floor. Peter was huge and extraordinarily handsome with a smooth face that looked as though it had been polished with black boot polish. He played the guitar and sometimes came downstairs to join Richard and Pauline for what they called 'jam sessions' when they would choose a theme or a progression of chords and take it in turn to play variations. Now Richard was composing some divertimenti for oboe, piano and guitar. They had all tried to persuade me to learn the flute but I knew my limitations and refused. Joe, the other Nigerian, was smaller and quieter, and he did not play a musical instrument either. He was very sensitive, and got terribly upset whenever he came across any colour prejudice, but Peter just roared with laughter. At first I was surprised that Mrs. Thomson was not prejudiced for she struck me as the sort of person who easily might be but she merely laughed comfortably and said: 'We're all Jock Tamson's bairns, black or white.' She said it very often and I think she was rather proud of her broadmindedness.

This afternoon she did not hear me come in and I reached my room in safety. When I first moved in it had been, in Richard's words, 'All chocolate brown paint and sick green curtains.' I had had to leave the brown paint but now I had gay orange curtains and Mrs. Thomson had allowed us to cover the faded pink flowery wallpaper with clean white emulsion paint. And Peter had given me a beautifully gawdy piece of material woven in Nigeria to cover up my divan bed. If ever I had enough money I

7

planned further improvements, a new lampshade, a sheepskin rug and some scatter cushions.

Still, it was my own room and though I would never like it as much as my room on Stranday or my room in the high house, I was beginning to feel at home in it.

I took off my school blazer and hung it behind the door, lit my gas fire, drew the curtains and took the stores into the kitchen.

I did not like the kitchen; it was small with torn brown patterned lino on the floor, a gas stove which I simply could not get clean, and chocolate brown cupboards. It always seemed to smell of gas and decayed vegetables, though I opened the window regularly and sprayed it with aerosol.

I put on the kettle and while it was boiling I scrubbed four potatoes and put them in the oven to bake in their jackets. I made myself a mug of coffee, spread a piece of brown bread with butter and honey and returned to my room.

Richard was not home yet. If I was sensible I would polish off some of my homework before he arrived. But I felt too weary. And at this time of day I particularly missed Aunt Patsy and Stephen and my darling little cousin Vanessa (who would be one in March) and my life on the island.

I shut my eyes and imagined myself in the cottage kitchen, which, if seldom tidy, was always clean and welcoming. There would be a peat fire burning and I would be able to hear the wind in the trees and the gentle swish of the sea. I loved living on Stranday, but the island school did not take people further than O-levels and rather than go and live in a hostel at Oban I had decided to come back to Edinburgh and take my Highers at Parkhill. Stephen and Patsy were both painters so that they could work anywhere but I, unfortunately, was not artistic and would have to earn my living in a more conventional way. I was hoping to leave school immediately after taking my Highers and go to Edinburgh University to study history and possibly archaeology. It would depend how good my marks were but I thought I might get A's for History and English, and B's for French and Geography if I worked hard.

But it was very difficult to combine working hard with cooking, shopping and keeping the flat clean, quite apart from the fact that I was often beguiled to join in the musical evenings next door and to prepare endless cups of coffee for Richard and his friends. Pauline, Richard's girlfriend, was very nice but she was not exactly the domestic type and though she always promised to do the washing up she was quite likely to forget.

And then there was Alastair, the most distracting influence of the lot.

I had met him during the summer on the island where he and I were both taking part in an archaeological dig and had fallen desperately in love with him. The trouble was that although he kissed me and told me how nice I was he never actually said that he loved me too. At times I felt sure that he did and at others I was torn by doubts. I was far from beautiful, not particularly clever and lacking, I felt, in all those qualities contained in the word sex-appeal—mystery, glamour and magnetism. And he was nineteen, three years older than I was.

Now he was in his second year at Glasgow University, studying archaeology and living at home. His father, who was a shipyard worker, had suddenly lost his job in the middle of the summer and Alastair had had to hurry home to get a holiday job navvying to help out. So what with overtime and weekend work and settling in for his new term he had had little time to come through to Edinburgh and had not specifically invited me to Glasgow. We wrote letters, of course, but Alastair, unfortunately, was not a gifted letter writer; he wrote about his work, what the foreman said, the weather, but in between the 'Darling Emma' at the beginning and the 'All my love, Alastair' at the end there was little in them resembling the sort of love letter I really longed for.

I had finished my coffee and my bread and honey. I took out my French books, put them on the table in front of the window and considered doing my homework. But I kept imagining Alastair's face, a thin rather spiky face with clear bright grey eyes and a shaggy mop of dark hair. And he would be saying: 'Dear Emma, nice Emma, oh I wish we had more time together.' Time was always so terribly short. He had spent one Saturday with me and it seemed that almost before I had been fully conscious of the joy in being together I had been kissing him goodbye at Waverley Station. I relived every minute of that day now—meeting him off the train when he hugged me till I was breathless; bringing him home for lunch with Richard and Pauline; taking him for a walk in the Meadows. But the best time had been in the evening in my room when I had sat leaning against his knees while he stroked my hair, kissed me from time to time, and we reminisced about summer on the island and made plans for going there together at Christmas.

I heard the front door crash and then footsteps coming up the stairs. It would be Richard coming home. It was six o'clock and I hadn't done a stroke of homework. Now I should have to get supper ready.

2

I listened more carefully and realised that Pauline was with him too. I mentally divided the four potatoes between three and realised that we would have to fill up with bread and cheese. I felt unreasonably annoyed; unreasonably because Pauline was not at all interested in food and would be perfectly content with a cup of coffee and a sandwich.

Although I liked her, at the same time I was envious of her because she and Richard could be together whenever they wanted—while Alastair was fifty miles away. And I envied her her looks and her charm. She had hair the colour, Richard said, of golden syrup and whatever she wore, however ridiculous, always looked right and gay. She wore bell-bottomed trousers in unusual colours, men's shirts, or frilly blouses, enormous ear-rings, a patchwork skirt, beaded moccasins, knee-high boots and a huge black cloak lined with emerald green, all with equal aplomb while I only looked nice in conventional attire and I had no money to spare for experiments.

At the moment I was wearing my school uniform, white shirt, school tie, navy-blue skirt and 'sensible' shoes, and I wished I'd changed.

Theoretically no one in the house was supposed to have a guest of the opposite sex in his or her room but naturally Mrs. Thomson's rules did not apply to Pauline. She called her 'Mrs. T.', brought her bunches of flowers, teased her about being a merry widow, knew the names and occupations of her sons and daughters and was always happy to discuss whether Tom would be right to emigrate to Canada and whether Betty should have her third baby at home or in hospital.

Now she knocked on my door and stuck her pretty, lively face into my room.

'Hullo, Emma.'

'Hullo,' I grunted.

'I've brought a surprise for you.'

'A surprise?'

Pauline, being the only child of rather rich parents, had a good deal more money than either Richard or myself and she loved giving presents. And I loved receiving them though I found it difficult to do so gracefully. I found it particularly difficult at the moment since I had just been resenting sharing my potato with her.

She handed me a large brown paper parcel and in it was a garment in soft brown wool, rather like a monk's robe, with long sleeves and a hood.

'For working in the long cold winter evenings,' said Pauline, delightedly, watching my face to see my reaction. 'Do try it on.'

I knew instinctively that I was going to look a buffoon.

'Later,' I mumbled. 'I must finish my homework.'

'No, now,' insisted Pauline.

I gritted my teeth, feeling crosser and crosser and

more and more ashamed of being ungrateful.

'Oh, all right.'

'Come and show when you're ready,' said Pauline, delicately retiring.

I took off my school clothes and slipped the monk's habit over my head. I knotted the white woollen girdle round my waist and put up the hood. It felt amazingly warm and comfortable, and when I looked in the mirror I didn't look a buffoon at all, just rather unusual.

I paraded up and down the room, the soft stuff swishing round my ankles. It was lovely but I hoped it had not been too expensive. No amount of telling myself that Pauline had plenty of money and that sometimes it is more blessed to receive than give could prevent my embarrassment. Richard never minded at all when Pauline paid for meals in restaurants or tickets to cinemas and concerts, but that, I supposed, was because he was in love with her. But I liked strict reciprocity as far as money and food and presents were concerned.

Still, I put on my best smile and as much enthusiasm into my voice as I could and went next door to show off and thank Pauline.

'It's marvellous,' I said. 'You really shouldn't.'

'Do you honestly like it?' asked Pauline. 'You look great in it, doesn't she, Richard?'

'Why do monks have so much nicer clothes than nuns?' queried Richard. 'No one would have thanked you for a nun's outfit.'

'Yes, they have to shave their hair, poor darlings,' said Pauline, running her fingers through her shining locks.

'I'll get supper,' I said.

'I'll help,' said Pauline.

'No, I'll do it.' It was the least I could do.

'I'll help,' repeated Pauline.

'You must stop being such a little martyr,' reproved Richard.

'Well, you lay the table,' I snapped at him.

I allowed Pauline to cut the cabbage, while I put ham, potatoes, butter, cheese, bread and honey on the tray. Fortunately Peter and Joe tended to eat late in the evening so we did not often quarrel over the use of the kitchen. But they had a horrid habit of leaving saucepans to soak.

Supper was a pleasant meal though I could not entirely get rid of my gloom at being so far away from Aunt Patsy and Stephen and from Alastair.

'Got the glumps?' asked Pauline, sympathetically. She tended to use ridiculous made-up words and this was a favourite, being a combination of gloom and dumps.

'A bit,' I said.

Richard and Pauline were so happy together that they did not really need me and like Pauline's presents I sometimes felt that they were being consciously 'nice' to me because I was younger and on my own.

'Stay and listen to some music,' Pauline suggested, but that was not at all what I felt like. I wanted Alastair to appear from nowhere and say all the things I wanted him to say, like I love you, and let's get married though I knew perfectly well that to get married at sixteen before I had finished school would be ridiculous and foolish. But I felt I had been sensible for years and years and it would be such a pleasant change to be foolish.

I left them, both promising to do the washing up, and

15

started to write an essay on the Jesuits. At least, in my monk's habit, I was deliciously warm.

I heard the piano and the oboe start up next door playing one of Richard's weird compositions. At first I had liked his music but now it had become very strange and cacophonic. He dismissed his earlier stuff as 'juvenile lyricism' and spoke about 'total thematisation' and other grandiloquent phrases. Loneliness pressed upon me.

I had looked forward to meeting people at school but my friend Elizabeth had changed. She now went around with a boy called Nigel and only wanted to talk about what he had said or done or intended to do.

All her free evenings she kept for him.

The others seemed to be in either pairs or groups in which I didn't fit. Why had I allowed myself to be persuaded into staying at school when I could still have been on the island, helping with the gallery, looking after Vanessa and feeling loved and needed? Aunt Patsy wouldn't have minded. She despised education. It was only Richard and Stephen who had been determinedly against my leaving. And then I remembered. It had really been Alastair's influence that had made me change my mind, because when I was on the dig with him people had called me 'Alastair's little lamb' and I'd realised I always would be unless I developed interests of my own. I had got to stick this year out because of Alastair.

But suppose he did not really love me and had only been flattered by my adoration? He must be meeting all sorts of girls, more beautiful and intelligent than I was. Probably he was trying tactfully to withdraw.

'Emma! Emma!'

In the distance I heard Mrs. Thomson's voice. What could she be wanting?

Resignedly I hauled myself to my feet and opened my door.

'What is it?'

'Telephone, my lassie. It's your young man.'

I floated down the stairs to where Mrs. Thomson stood beaming.

'I said to myself, that'll cheer the lassie up.'

'Thanks, Mrs. Thomson.'

I seized the receiver from her hand and said breathlessly:

'Hullo, Alastair.'

'I'm so glad you're in. I thought you might be out on the town. It's good news. My Dad has got another job.'

'Oh good. Oh I am glad.'

'General relaxation all round. So what about you coming to Glasgow this weekend? You could come early on Saturday and stay the night.'

'Oh Alastair, I'd love to.'

'I could pay your fare.'

'No, it's all right.'

I wouldn't have my winter dress cleaned and I'd mend my tights instead of buying new ones.

'Are you missing me? Or have you forgotten me?'

'I've forgotten you.'

'Are you fine otherwise?'

'Absolutely fine. Pauline's just given me a monk's habit.'

'Well, don't wear it at the weekend. I don't go for monks.'

'I'll catch the nine o'clock train, shall I?'

'Yes, and I'll meet you at Queen Street.'

'Lovely.'

'Can you hear that?'

'What?'

'It's a kiss. More to follow.'

Oh darling, darling Alastair. I danced back up the stairs and interrupted Richard and Pauline.

'That was Alastair. I'm going to Glasgow at the weekend. You'll have to do the cooking, Pauline.'

'Oh Lord!' said Richard rudely.

'I don't care,' I said happily, 'you can both starve.'

'I'm so glad,' said Pauline spontaneously and I wanted to hug her.

'Now I'm going to finish my essay and tomorrow I shall do my English interpretation and my French translation and then, on Saturday—' I whirled out of the room.

I looked at myself in the mirror again and sighed. Last summer, before I went abroad with Richard, for the first and only time in my life I'd had my hair professionally cut and set in a hairdresser's shop. It had grown again. It was almost what Richard and I called my 'highland cattle cut' and I had to look beautiful for Alastair. I had got used to it being curly and red (or auburn, or bronze or copper or any of the politer words), but now it was neither long nor short, simply messy.

'Pauline,' I called, 'before I do anything else you must cut my hair.'

3

Diddly dump, diddly dump, sang the diesel train and then Hoo-hoo, a sound that is so eerie at night but on this bright frosty morning, on the way to Glasgow to meet Alastair, so gay and triumphant. I wanted to sing back Hoo-hoo, but of course I didn't. Instead I looked out of the window at tidy fields, grey woollen sheep clustered together to keep warm, almost leafless woods, hills radiant in the clear air. Autumn air, I thought, is blue and gives the landscape a soft glow, just as summer air is gold and spring air is pale green. And winter air is absolutely transparent and colourless. I had brought a newspaper to read because Alastair (unlike Richard and Pauline) was politically well-informed and liked to discuss what was happening and why. But I could not concentrate and after a few headlines had gone into one side of my head and re-appeared out of the other without leaving a trace of meaning, I gave up and simply enjoyed my feelings of anticipation.

Even the outskirts of Glasgow, the grim skyscraper flats, the piles of rubble and the mean black suburban houses failed to depress me.

At least ten minutes before the train drew in to Queen

Street station I had combed my hair, adjusted my make-up, zipped up my jacket and was standing by the door ready to leap out the moment the train stopped. But I did not run up the platform, I walked sedately to the barrier, searching among the people, waiting for Alastair's dark head. Yes, he was there, waving furiously and in a second I was in his arms. How splendid that he was not one of those reticent Scots who do not approve of embracing in public.

'Emma! How lovely.'

'Alastair!'

'Let me look at you.'

I wanted to look at him too. Somehow when you have not seen someone for several weeks but have had thousands of imaginary conversations with him you feel quite shy and need several minutes to adjust your imaginary picture to the real person. So we stared at each other, almost at arms' length and then suddenly Alastair laughed, tucked my arm through his and we walked out of the station.

Student fashions seem to change from year to year if not from month to month. At one time all the Edinburgh students had worn huge duffel coats and long college scarves; then they had all worn jeans, sneakers and big fishermen's jerseys; this year it was what the magazines called 'the furry look' and Alastair was wearing a shaggy jacket that looked as though it had once been used for an arctic expedition. And his hair was longer than I had ever seen it though thank goodness he had not grown a beard.

I had never spent more than a few hours in Glasgow

between trains but the first thing that always struck me was the starlings. All the part near Queen Street simply reverberated with the squawks of thousands and thousands of starlings perched on the high black buildings.

'Let's have some coffee,' said Alastair, leading the way into a small steamy café. We sat on opposite sides of such a narrow table that our knees touched and then suddenly I wasn't shy any more and we began to talk. First I had a refreshing grumble about my housekeeping problems, Richard and Pauline's thoughtlessness, Mrs. Thomson's fussing but I was able to make it sound funny so that Alastair laughed as well as making sympathetic comments.

And he told me what a miserable couple of months he had had because his father hated being out of work. He just sat around looking gloomy until his mother told him to 'snap out of it' and then they both quarrelled.

'Then,' said Alastair, 'she'd offer him five bob and tell him to go to the pub and get out of her road. But Dad won't spend money on beer when he's not earning and he'd just sink farther back into his chair and switch the television off and on until we all nearly went mad.'

'But it's all right now?'

'Yes, the shipyard's got an order for some Polish trawlers and Dad goes back on the job on Monday. It's an extraordinary thing, Emma, but when he's gloomy he seems to shrink in size. They want to meet you, by the way, so I'm taking you home for dinner.'

At this I had more than a slight feeling of alarm. I suppose any girl does when she has to meet her boyfriend's parents for the first time. Would they like me?

Would I like them? I knew very little about them except that Alastair's father was dead keen on education. In which case he might consider that I was a distracting influence. And I knew Alastair was devoted to his mother which might mean that she resented his girlfriends automatically.

'Don't look so worried, Emma, they won't eat you. They're just ordinary nice rather old-fashioned people.'

He squeezed my hand so I pulled myself together and we began to talk again, about our work, about how much we had missed each other.

'Honestly Alastair, I was sitting in my monk's habit writing about the Jesuits—'

'How suitable.'

'And feeling as though a dozen black dogs were crouched on my shoulders when darling Mrs. Thomson called up to me that you were on the telephone.'

'Now things are back to normal I'll ring you up more often. In a way I'm scared to, in case you're out because then I'd be so disappointed.'

'I'm hardly ever out.'

'Now look just because you wear a monk's habit it doesn't mean you've got to behave like a nun. Haven't you got friends?'

'Not at the moment. What do you do in the evenings?'

'Oh this and that,' said Alastair carelessly, 'beer with the boys, the pictures and I've joined the Socialist Society so that means the odd meeting or lecture.'

I badly wanted to ask who he went to the pictures with but it might sound as though I was jealous. Alastair was the sort of cheerful, sociable character who always had dozens of friends, I knew, and I liked him that way but all the same I could not help feeling the tiniest twinge of loneliness and left-out-ness at the thought of him gallivanting round Glasgow while I sat alone in my room. I remembered how jealous I'd been of that girl on the dig, last summer, Nancy her name was. She'd made enormous efforts to attract Alastair, but, here I cheered up, he hadn't been in the least impressed. If he preferred me to the fascinating Nancy perhaps I was safe after all.

'Come on,' said Alastair, 'we'll walk around for a while and then take the bus to my place. Dinner's at half past twelve.'

His parents had recently been re-housed and now they lived in an almost brand-new block of flats. It was all very bright and clean and convenient, Alastair said, with central heating and parquet floors but his mother missed her neighbours and the shops were miles away. But the worst thing was the lack of sound-proofing.

'The chap next door's alarm clock goes off as if it were beside my bed,' said Alastair gloomily, 'and what's more he sets it for 5.30 in the morning.'

'How awful.'

'We put our radio on to drown the radio next door and then they turn theirs up and so we turn ours up and so on and so on till you can't hear yourself think.'

'I like old houses best,' I said and I laughed to myself to remember how horrified I'd been when I first came to live with Aunt Patsy and discovered she lived at the top of a crumbling tenement just off Edinburgh's Royal Mile. Then I'd thought that old houses were terrible and that people only lived in them because they could not afford new ones.

I told Alastair about this, adding: 'I was the most awful little prig,' and I described my abortive efforts to reform Aunt Patsy and make her respectable.

Alastair was tickled to death and he told me what he'd been like at that age, obsessed with passing exams so that he could go to a good school, never going out to play until he'd finished his homework, being teased by the other boys because he was 'teacher's pet'.

'Perhaps we're both nicer now,' he suggested.

'I hope so.' But I knew he had always been nice.

Alastair's block of flats was on concrete stilts and underneath children were playing with tricycles and skipping ropes, older ones were wheeling babies in prams or staggering home with bags bursting with potatoes and loaves of bread.

We pushed open a heavy metal-framed door and went into the dimly lit hall-way where there were four doors at each corner with people's names on. We stepped into the lift and sailed slowly up to the ninth floor.

'Don't look so nervous, Emma,' said Alastair, kissing me.

I wished for the thousandth time I had a new winter coat. I was wearing a dark brown skirt and, since I had been encouraged to wear things the same colour as my hair, an orange jersey. But over this comparatively respectable outfit I had to wear my old anorak which had spent a year on the island and looked it.

'I'm not at all nervous,' I snapped, 'it's just that I don't like lifts.'

'I do,' said Alastair, kissing me again.

We stepped out into another identical dimly lit hall and approached door number 37. Outside on a neat black plate was the name Munro in white. Alastair fished into the letter box where the latch key hung on a string and opened the door. A rich smell of cooking and furniture polish came out to meet us.

Alastair put his head into the kitchen and called: 'We're here, Mum.'

A small dark woman with an anxious face came towards us, wiping her hands on her apron.

'This is Emma, Mum.'

'Pleased to meet you,' said Mrs. Munro.

'Thank you very much for inviting me,' I mumbled.

'Take her into the sitting room to meet Dad,' said Mrs. Munro, 'I'm just finishing up in here.'

Alastair helped me off with my jacket and hung it up in the hall and then I followed him into the sitting room.

Mr. Munro was so like Alastair that I liked him immediately; he had the same dark hair though it was going a little grey at the sides, and the same sparkling eyes and on him Alastair's spiky features had become rather impressive and craggy.

He shook hands vigorously and ushered me into what was clearly the best chair. Then he offered me a cigarette.

'I don't smoke, thank you.'

'Sensible girl,' he approved.

I sat with my legs neatly side by side and looked round the room. It was tidy with green curtains and green and white flowered wallpaper; plaster birds were fixed to the wall and there was a tinted wedding photograph on the sideboard. There was a small bookcase which held the

25

collected works of Walter Scott.

Then I understood about the soundproofing for from one side I could hear someone laboriously practising scales on the piano and from underneath came the indistinct throb of the radio.

'Are you coming to the game this afternoon?' Mr. Munro asked Alastair, 'you could bring your friend.'

'I don't think so,' said Alastair. 'Dad's a Partick Thistle supporter,' he added to me.

I smiled wanly but I had no intention of wasting a precious afternoon watching football.

Alastair picked up a newspaper and Mr. Munro and I stared at each other, trying to think of something to say.

'So you're the girl who lives on an island,' he said at last.

'Well, I used to but I'm in Edinburgh now,' I explained, 'because there's no secondary school on the island.'

'And you're taking your Highers?'

'Yes.'

'Good for you, good for you,' said Mr. Munro heartily.

The sitting room was joined to the kitchen by sliding glass doors and now Mrs. Munro opened these and began laying the table. I jumped up to help her but she motioned me away.

'No, no, you sit down.'

'Is dinner ready, Mum, I've got to be out of the house at the back of one,' said Mr. Munro, looking at his watch.

'You and your football, you're like a bairn,' complained Mrs. Munro, placing dishes on the table. 'And where's Derek?'

'We're not waiting for Derek.'

So we sat down and I was helped to stew, potatoes and cabbage which I had to keep assuring Mrs. Munro was delicious and exactly what I liked.

Then Derek, Alastair's eleven-year-old brother, wearing jeans and a torn jersey, erupted into the room. When he saw me he blushed scarlet and did not say a word but he kept watching me while he shovelled in his stew and potatoes.

Afterwards there were stewed apples and custard but Mr. Munro, looking at his watch again, said he couldn't stop for it or he'd be late, he'd see us later some time.

Derek gulped his and also rose to his feet and spoke his first sentence.

'I'm away out, Mum,' he said and vanished with a slam of the door.

Mrs. Munro sighed. 'I don't like those laddies he goes around with,' she said. 'They play in those half-demolished buildings and it's not safe.'

'He'll be all right, Mum.'

'He's not like what you were at that age, Alastair. He was always a laddie to have his nose in a book,' she said to me, 'but this one won't read anything above a comic. I have to tie him to his chair to get his homework done.'

'Don't fuss,' said Alastair.

'If I don't his father will.'

She began to clear away and again I offered to help but was refused. So Alastair and I sat in front of the electric fire and drank tea. I was excruciatingly bored. If I had been like Pauline I would perhaps have been able to get the conversation going but though I racked

27

and racked my brains I could think of absolutely nothing to say. And Alastair was no help at all. So I just sat there, listening to the clatter of crockery as Mrs. Munro did the washing up and to the radio below and what I imagined was the television next door for people who preferred to see their football matches in comfort. Now Alastair got up and switched their set on.

'Shall we watch the sports programme?' he asked.

I was so filled with outrage that I could not speak. Watch the television on the only afternoon we had had together for weeks! He couldn't mean it. I glowered at him but he was looking at the screen and not at me. Ostentatiously I picked up the newspaper and found the TV programmes—football preview, international hockey, racing, a football match, wrestling ... —it filled up the whole afternoon. Was Alastair really going to sit and watch the whole thing?

Alastair looked up at me and smiled. Then he patted the place on the sofa beside him. 'Come and sit beside me,' he invited.

Now I had read all about girls who pretended to share the interests of their boyfriends and it only landed them into further difficulties—a lifetime of watching sport on the telly for instance, or shivering on football grounds. It was definitely not for me.

But that smile and the thought of sitting with his arm round me was hard to resist. After all, I needn't actually watch. I would make it clear at a later date that I was not and never would be the slightest bit interested in sport. So I joined him on the sofa.

His arm came round me as I knew it would and he

gave me delicate warm kisses somewhere between my eyebrow and my hair.

Without moving his eyes from the screen where some game—I think it was hockey—was being played he breathed into my ear: 'I love you.'

I closed my eyes with joy and the programme flickered on.

4

'Well, now you know how the workers live,' said Alastair when, after more tea and biscuits, we eventually left the house in order to go to the pictures.

I did not quite know how to take this remark. I was never quite sure where I came in the social scale because my life had been so completely divided into two. Until I was thirteen (when my parents had been killed in a car crash) I had lived very conventionally in a London suburb. My father worked in the legal department of an insurance office and my mother stayed at home. We had a car and a garden and three weeks' holiday every summer and life was happy and uneventful. But when I came to live with Aunt Patsy all this changed. Although she was mother's sister she was different in every way. She lived in what I can only describe politely as picturesque squalor, forgot about mealtimes; she was either too poor to send any laundry or so rich that she bought flowers and gramophone records and bottles of wine; she went out shopping (when she remembered) in trousers and a paint-stained jersey and was quite likely to have paint on her face as well; she often worked all night and I would come home from school to find her eating breakfast at tea-time. At first I had been desperately unhappy and it was only because we became extremely fond of one another that we were able to make allowances for our different habits and temperaments—I tried to be a little less methodical and Aunt Patsy a little more and though we still squabbled and complained it was mostly good-humoured; Stephen, who stood about half-way between us, used to keep us in order by, as he put it, bashing our pretty little heads together.

I realised that Alastair's parents were as conventional as mine had been in a different way and that I would just have to accept them. I did not care a fig if they were working class or middle class so long as I was not involved in a way of life I did not like. Alastair had behaved so naturally with Aunt Patsy and Stephen that it had given me quite a shock to see a different side to him, as the son of the house being waited on by his mother, watching the television and being interested in football.

As we hailed a bus and climbed in I decided to ask him a few questions.

'Do you often go to football matches with your father?'

'Now and again.'

'Would you have gone if I hadn't been here?'

'Probably. But I thought it would be cosier on the sofa. It was, wasn't it?'

'Mmm.'

'Did you like my Mum and Dad?'

'Of course.'

'You were very quiet.'

'I always find it difficult to talk to new people.'

'I think they were a bit scared of you, coming from an

artistic background and all that. What were your real parents like, Emma?'

I gulped. I had never talked about them to anyone. At first it had been so painful that I simply couldn't and then silence had become a habit. I thought of them when I was lonely or unhappy but gradually they had become misty, insubstantial people. What is more I had changed so much myself that I wondered, with a little shock, if I would now know what to talk to them about.

'I'm sorry,' said Alastair, after a pause. 'I don't want to hurt you. But it is interesting.'

'Some other time,' I mumbled.

'Of course. I'm always putting my foot into it, aren't I?'

'It's not that. It's just that I never do.'

'Have you heard from your aunt lately?' he asked, changing the subject.

'Yes. The gallery roof has been leaking again and Vanessa can crawl and stand up and Stephen is going to have an exhibition in Glasgow in the spring and—oh you will be able to come for Christmas, won't you Alastair? If Richard's car holds out he might drive us up to Oban.'

'I'll try,' said Alastair, 'or you could come here.'

Oh no, I thought, oh no, I will not spend Christmas being bored at no. 37.

'New Year is best though,' went on Alastair not noticing, I hope, my dismayed expression, 'we have a real houseful and a sing-song and everything. It's great. You'd love it.'

'I'm sure I would,' I said with an effort. But I was still absolutely determined to go to the island.

I looked out of the window and wondered why Glasgow

was so different from Edinburgh. Of course it was much, much bigger and the houses were blacker, but there was also a different atmosphere; the lights looked murkier, the streets were more crowded; the people looked smaller and more in a hurry. We were bowling along an endless street packed with tiny shops and every fifth one seemed to be a pub with a garish neon sign saying 'Joe's Bar' or something. And the conductor called me 'hen'. But above all I felt the throbbing excitement of a big over-populated industrial city set for Saturday night enjoyment. I asked Alastair what the difference was and he said:

'Glasgow's warmer, more alive. Edinburgh's cold and windy and full of toffee-nosed people.'

'What nonsense!' I said indignantly, for though I had similar feelings when I first arrived in Edinburgh now I was deeply attached to the city.

'This is where we get off,' said Alastair, taking my elbow protectively.

At the cinema I took out my purse and whispered, 'I'll pay my share.'

'You will not. When I take a girl out I take a girl out.'

He looked at me furiously as if I had offered him the direst insult.

He bought the tickets and a packet of sweets and stumped angrily ahead.

It was rather like diving into a dark scented pool; the usherettes swam about with lighted torches; there were ripples of whispered conversation; and grey clouds of cigarette smoke were blown by invisible waves.

We settled down in our seats but Alastair sat bolt upright glaring straight ahead. He was angry with me.

'Alastair,' I whispered, 'I'm sorry. I didn't mean to hurt your feelings. It's just that—well, I've hardly been out with a boy before.'

Alastair smiled and slid an arm round my shoulders. Then with his other hand he took mine.

Holding hands at the cinema—I'd read about it and talked about it and only a short time ago I had thought it an extremely foolish way of behaving and sworn that I would never do so. And now little waves of delicious sensation spread all over my body as Alastair stroked the back of my wrist with his thumb, traced a pattern on my palm and gently separated each finger in turn. Our heads were so close that I could feel the warmth emanating from his cheek. We looked at each other and the light from the screen was reflected in his eyes.

'Darling,' he murmured.

'Darling,' I murmured back.

I can't remember what the film was about. I had a vague impression of some beautiful girl wearing beautiful clothes; people getting in and out of cars; lighting cigarettes, pouring drinks, going up and down in lifts, visiting or coming away from huge apartments; there was love, misunderstanding and reconciliation. I compared the hero unfavourably with Alastair and myself unfavourably with the heroine.

Then the lights went up and we staggered drunkenly out into the street.

When we got back to no. 37, Mrs. Munro was putting cheese and oatcakes on the table. Derek was sprawled on the sofa with a comic and Mr. Munro was striding up and down describing the football match. In the background the television (and the television next door) flickered and mumbled.

'Come and have your supper,' said Mrs. Munro.

We all sat down and Mr. Munro went through the game blow by blow for Alastair's benefit. Partick Thistle had lost and Mr. Munro blamed the goal-keeper, the referee and some character called Connaught who was a lousy forward.

Alastair, who apparently knew each member of the team as if they were his brothers, gave a highly technical description of their strengths and shortcomings.

'Football, football,' sighed Mrs. Munro at intervals.

I did not say anything except 'Thank you' and 'Would you pass the butter please'.

Eventually it was time for bed. One end of the sofa was pulled down to make a bed and Mrs. Munro brought sheets and blankets, fussing over whether I would be comfortable and warm enough. When they had all disappeared I undressed, turned off the fire, and got into bed. I could hear the murmur of voices, the sounds of cisterns re-filling, lorries changing gear as they chugged along the road outside, the distant hoot of a diesel.

And I was filled with doubts and misgivings. At some moments Alastair and I had been so close we had almost been one person. And then he had seemed to disappear and become a complete stranger. Was being in love always like this, I wondered. Richard and Pauline always seemed so happy and at ease together. They argued from time to time but they certainly had no such divergent interests as Alastair and I had about football.

Then there was a slight knock at the door and Alastair came in.

'I didn't say goodnight properly,' he whispered, kneeling beside the bed and kissing me.

My doubts disappeared. Being in love was marvellous.

5

Coming home in the overheated diesel I attempted to sort out my reactions to the weekend. I had woken up early and for once the flat was absolutely quiet. The trouble is that when I wake up I like to get up immediately. I always feel hungry and full of energy. But here it might not be polite. Still, I could at least get dressed and re-assemble the sofa. Surely no one would mind if I went very quietly into the kitchen and made myself a cup of coffee. I was just doing this when Alastair had appeared, looking tousled and sleepy.

'You are an early bird,' he said.

'I always am.'

'We'll have breakfast together, shall we?'

'I'll get it ready.'

'Can you find things?'

'Of course.'

'All right. I'll shave.'

So we had had a nice cosy breakfast together and then, when Mrs. Munro appeared cluck-clucking because guests weren't supposed to get their own breakfasts, Alastair told her we were going out for the day.

'Well, come back in time for your dinner at four,' she said.

So Alastair and I took the suburban train to Balloch which is on the shores of Loch Lomond. Although it was a grey cloudy day and extremely cold I could see that the loch deserved its reputation for beauty. Wild wooded mountains rose on either side and there was a cap of snow on top of Ben Lomond. The loch itself was whipped into white-topped waves by the wind. We walked up the eastern shore road to a place called Rowardennan and there it began to rain so we went into the hotel and Alastair drank beer and I drank cider and we munched a great number of potato crisps.

'We'll come again in the summer and go out in a boat,' said Alastair.

'Do let's,' I agreed enthusiastically.

Back at no. 37 there was a huge meal waiting for us, roast pork, chips and peas, jam tarts and custard. After we had eaten Derek bolted out to play as usual and Mr. Munro and Alastair buried themselves in the Sunday papers.

This time I succeeded in helping Mrs. Munro clear away and wash up but when I returned to the sitting room I decided I did not want to read the papers or to watch the television. I wanted to go home. I had thought that just being in the same room as Alastair would be bliss enough but it wasn't. After some hesitation I said:

'Alastair.'

'Mmm?'

'I'd like to catch the half-past six train.'

'So early?'

'I've got to tidy up and iron my shirt and finish off my homework.'

Now, as the train slowed down before the Waverley tunnel I felt a little guilty. But after all, I defended myself, watching people read newspapers isn't fun. And there would probably have been another sports programme on the television or some ancient film about cowboys. And I did have to get the flat tidy for Monday morning. I would like to close my eyes and listen to some music or have a very gentle conversation with Richard and Pauline.

'Woo hoo,' I called as I went upstairs.

'Woo hoo,' came Richard's voice. I opened his door and went in. He was lying on the sofa, which was how, he said, he got his best ideas.

'Inspiration?' I asked respectfully.

'Not even a little straggled-tailed one. Come on. Did you have a good time?'

'Fabulous.'

'The course of true love running smooth?'

I hesitated. I did not want to tell a direct lie but I was not ready for confidences.

'Where's Pauline?' I asked instead.

'She wanted to go out and I wanted to stay in,' said Richard grumpily. 'Emma, you must teach her to cook, I've had the most repulsive food all weekend.'

I giggled. I couldn't help it.

'Alastair likes football,' I said. 'He made me watch the sports programme all Saturday afternoon.'

We both burst into peals of laughter.

'I'll cook you a Welsh rarebit and we'll have some coffee,' I said, going into the kitchen. Richard followed and leaned against the door while I told him about my weekend. Now I came to think of it it was very funny and I gave a spirited imitation of Mr. Munro describing the match.

'He must have a photographic memory,' said Richard.

'He's really very nice,' I said quickly.

'Of course. Now go on, tell me more.'

So feeling rather treacherous I continued my tale while Richard wolfed two enormous Welsh rarebits. At last he sighed and leaned back. 'That's better,' he said. 'The outer man is useless unless the inner man has been attended to. I've had an inspiration already. You remember those rounds we sang when we were on holiday.'

'Of course.'

'It has just struck me that you have a very fair voice. I don't mean you'll ever be a Kathleen Ferrier but you can sing in tune. Why don't I compose something for our little ensemble including the human voice, in fact yours?'

'Do you really think I could?'

'You could try.'

'But nothing all semi-tones and no tune,' I said suspiciously.

'You want me to return to my juvenile lyricism?'

'Yes.'

'Well find me a poem, something simple, Elizabethan perhaps.'

'I'd like some music now,' I said.

'I'm too tired and too full to play. I'll put a record on. What do you fancy?'

'That Bach thing, you know with the oboe and the

violin chasing each other and the harpsichord going chug, chug, chug.'

'An admirable description. You must write all my programme notes.'

6

It had taken me a little time to get used to Parkhill School again for I had forgotten all the irritating rules that are supposed to be necessary in a big school. On the island, everything was very free and easy. Nobody bothered about uniform and if the mini-bus which collected and took us to school was late Mr. Kilpatrick, the headmaster, knew it was Donald the Minbus's fault and not ours. He knew all of us personally, as did the other teachers, and no one accused us of being lazy if we were merely stupid.

But Parkhill was quite different. If you were late it was your own fault and you got a talking to from the headmaster and it was no good saying that the bus had been late or full up. Living in Marchmont I had to take two buses and at first I either used to arrive twenty minutes early or ten minutes late. Eventually I decided to walk unless it was pouring with rain because then I could gauge the time exactly.

Then, the Lady Adviser was always fussing about us being correctly dressed. She was the sort of person who considered anything fashionable to be a sign of delinquency. When long white socks were the rage she made us wear short ones. When dark stockings were fashionable she made us wear light ones (and vice versa) and she was always bustling about forcing the girls with long hair to tie it back, and issuing Kirby grips and india rubber bands. Her bête noire at the present time was short skirts. It was a hopeless battle, of course, for who was going to walk around in knee-length skirts when everyone else was wearing them several inches higher. But she did not give up easily. Standing in the upper or the lower hall, she would fix her gimlet gaze on the pupils coming up or down the stairs and pounce upon them with injunctions to 'get that skirt lengthened.'

'But it won't let down,' a girl would answer, or 'But my mother's just bought it for me, Miss Smith.'

'I don't want any excuses,' Miss Smith would bark. 'You can't go round looking like that.'

The girls who were forced into acquiring longer skirts used to hitch up the waistbands and then let them down suddenly if they saw Miss Smith hovering anywhere. And my friend, Elizabeth, who had long hair, seemed to spend a large part of her time putting it into rubber bands and taking it out again.

I had no trouble with my hair but my skirt really was rather short since I had grown upwards (if not outwards) and simply could not afford a new one. So I was always hiding in the cloakroom or hurrying down the passage hidden, I hoped, by bigger girls on either side.

For if she caught me she used to say dreadfully embarrassing things like:

'Now Emma, you come from a good home and you ought to know better,' or: 'It's up to girls like you to set an example.'

43

By 'girls like you' she meant that I did not smoke in the lavatories, use bad language or omit to do my homework.

I had also forgotten how horrible school dinners were, always overcooked and lukewarm, since they arrived by van in tin containers from some central depot. Some people went to the nearby café and bought buttered rolls, pies or bridies and I tried this once or twice. Others brought sandwiches and I tried this too. But there was nowhere comfortable to eat them in the cold weather.

Still the work itself was much more interesting. I had always liked the history teacher—and history was my favourite subject. And the new English teacher was young and modern and enthusiastic about creative writing—at least half the girls in the class were madly in love him.

Another nice thing was that the boys, whom we'd all considered as absolute morons when I was in second year, had miraculously grown up and were now almost civilised. They bought us bars of chocolate, invited us out to coffee, and even paid occasional compliments about our appearance. But if they wanted to take any of us out, the boy concerned would never ask direct. He would ask his friend to ask your friend if you would consider going out with him. That way they did not have their feelings hurt by a refusal.

So Elizabeth said to me one day at break:

'John asked Nigel to ask me to ask you if you'd like to go to a party on Saturday night.'

This was quite a feather in my cap because John was in sixth year, good-looking and with a scooter. I had first noticed him in the school choir, of which I was now a member, when he had been called out to sing the solo verses in 'The Holly and the Ivy'. I suppose he must have noticed me too because he began chatting to me after the practice.

'At last an alto who can hold her part,' he said flatteringly.

'Thank you very much.'

'You're new, aren't you?'

'Not brand new. I've been away for two years.'

'I thought I recognised you because of your—'

'Don't say "distinctive appearance" just say "red hair" —I'm used to it.'

'I like red hair,' said John.

So I was not entirely surprised at Elizabeth's message and for a moment I was quite tempted to say yes. Then I remembered that Alastair might phone.

'It's a bit difficult,' I said regretfully.

'Why?'

'My boyfriend might be coming this weekend.'

'Alastair?'

'Who else? I spent last weekend with him in Glasgow and had a fabulous time and now it's his turn to come here.'

'Would you go out with him through the week? John, I mean.'

'No, I'd better not. It might get complicated.'

I remembered Alastair saying that he didn't expect me to behave like a nun, but all the same. As far as I could make out if you went out with one boy it was taken for granted that you were a couple and I did not want to be a couple with anyone except Alastair. On the other hand

I liked the idea of a party.

'Are you going to the party?' I asked.

'Yes, I'm going with Nigel. It won't be an orgy if that's what you mean, we just sit around and yatter and play records.'

'I wasn't imagining it would be an orgy,' I said haughtily, though I had heard about parties where all the couples sat on each other's knees in the dark and the unattached people either had to stand in the kitchen or sit in melancholy solitude on the stairs.

It was no fun staying home every evening waiting for Alastair to phone. Richard was in one of his moods, though whether it was inspiration or bad temper I could not be sure. Pauline did not come round and when I asked him what she was up to he snapped:

'I haven't the faintest idea.'

So I sat in my monk's habit reading with my ears strained for the telephone, wishing I had enjoyed my weekend in Glasgow more. Perhaps I had offended Alastair by not being interested in football?

I found a poem for Richard—it was the charming sad love poem written by Henry the Eighth. I had always imagined that someone who hopped from one wife to another, divorcing or chopping off the heads of the ones he was tired of, would not be tender-hearted. But the poem sounded sincere.

> Whereto should I express
> My inward heaviness?
> No mirth can make me fain,
> Till that we meet again.

46

Do way, dear heart! Not so!
  Let no thought you dismay.
Though ye now part me fro,
  We shall meet when we may.

When I remember me
  Of your most gentle mind,
It may in no wise agree
  That I should be unkind.

The daisy delectable,
  The violet wan and blo,
Ye are not variable.
  I love you and no mo.

I make you fast and sure.
  It is to me great pain
Thus long to endure
  Till that we meet again.

Perhaps it was true that though his marriages had been only political he had really loved Jane Seymour tenderly and steadfastly.

No mirth can make me fain, till that we meet again, I murmured to myself, thinking of Alastair.

'Rather peculiar grammar,' said Richard, in a surly manner, but he took a piece of manuscript paper and began scribbling little black notes.

When I had practically given up hope Alastair rang on Friday evening. He sounded gay and affectionate.

'How's things?'

'Fine,' I said with false brightness.

47

'I keep remembering—' he paused significantly.

'Oh so do I.'

'Mum and Dad approve of you, by the way. They were afraid you'd be wearing beads and feathers.'

'Well, why not?'

'Oh you know. Like Pauline.'

'I think Pauline looks great.'

'I daresay she does for her but I wouldn't want you to dress like that.'

'Next time I'll come in my monk's habit,' I said curtly. Alastair laughed.

'And I shall grow a beard.'

'Oh no, Alastair.'

'Why not?'

'I was thinking of the feel rather than the look,' I said primly.

'Would it be like being cuddled by a grizzly bear?'

'It very well might.'

'I'm not going to really. What have you been doing?'

'Nothing much.'

'What *do* you do?'

'Read, listen to music, do my homework. I was asked to a party tomorrow by the way.'

'Good for you.'

'But I'm not going.'

'Why not?'

I was aghast. He ought to have known, to be pleased with my devotion.

'I thought you might be coming.'

'Sorry, chicken. But even if I were we could have gone together.'

48

He had obviously forgotten the code of behaviour at school. You couldn't be invited by one boy and turn up with another. It was Not Done.

And I was overcome by waves of disappointment. Alastair was not coming. I paused until he said:

'Are you still there?'

'Mm.'

'I was going to tell you. I'm a delegate to a conference this weekend, from the Socialist Society. It's on Civil Liberties, run by the United Nations Association. It should be interesting.'

I gulped.

'Greece and Northern Ireland and South Africa and so on,' went on Alastair, 'I may make a speech.'

'Fantastic,' I said in a hollow voice.

First football, then politics, when would he have time for me?

'So you go to your party as long as you don't let any tall, dark handsome men chat you up and take you home.'

I was silent again.

'Emma,' came Alastair's voice, 'you're not cross are you? Perhaps next weekend.'

I wanted to say 'Perhaps' and slam the phone down but that would be so final, especially since I couldn't ring him back.

So I swallowed the tears that threatened to engulf me and said airily:

'Cross? Of course not. See you sometime.'

'Sometime soon. Goodbye darling Emma,' and he rang off.

It was the most unsatisfactory telephone conversation

I had ever had in my life. He was perfectly happy dashing off to conferences and football matches and the pictures and I was perfectly miserable sitting alone in my room. And he didn't care. Not one atom.

Darling Emma, indeed, and remembering our kisses during the weekend! What hypocrisy! Why he had even been looking at that wretched hockey match when he told me that he loved me.

I walked upstairs like a sleepwalker, slowly and numbly, and then I threw myself on my bed and burst into tears.

7

That weekend, as I wasn't going to see Alastair and wasn't going to a party, I threw myself into domestic activity. I behaved to myself like those horrid mothers who say: 'I'll give you something to cry for if you don't stop crying.' I hoovered, swept, polished and dusted till I was exhausted. I scrubbed the nasty stove once again with steel wool and lashings of Vim. I took everything out of the food cupboard (not much, admittedly) and re-arranged it. I banished Richard to read in my room while I tackled his. He was furious.

'Emma, for goodness sake! Leave my room alone. It doesn't need cleaning. And you're not to touch my papers. Or anything.'

'You can't live knee-deep in muck,' I retorted. 'It's unhygienic. If you won't tidy it yourself then I shall. Now scram.'

Grumbling furiously Richard retired and, feeling like Hercules cleaning out the Augean stables, I set to work. The only place that escaped hot water and furniture polish was his working table as I knew if I touched that he would be unbearable for months. I polished the piano, filled sackfuls of crumpled manuscript paper, dusted and re-arranged the records; I washed curtains and cushion covers and hung them in the garden to dry; I discovered teaspoons, a fountain pen, several pencils, paper clips and a threepenny bit down the back of the sofa.

Pallid and smelling slightly of disinfectant, our rooms were at last clean to my satisfaction, and I put bread, cheese and tomatoes on a tray and went to rescue Richard. Self-righteousness had succeeded my gloom. Now I felt at one with all those women who spend their lives bending over hot stoves and working their fingers to the bone while their menfolk idled.

'I hope you're satisfied,' snarled Richard, 'now you've dislocated a good working day and ruined all inspiration probably for weeks.'

'Pooh inspiration,' I replied spiritedly. 'A typical excuse for laziness and lack of talent.'

'If you've touched the papers on my working table I shall strangle you.'

'I haven't. I have a little respect for your immortal works.'

'Actually,' said Richard, 'the song's fitting in quite well. I'm going to treat Peter's guitar as a lute and write virginal noises for the piano. And your voice and Pauline's oboe will chase each other. It'll be Elizabethan in form but very very contemporary in flavour. It's a pity you can't sing as loudly as an oboe. You must cultivate a nasal drawl.'

'Let's,' I said, 'when I've ironed the curtains and cushion covers, have a super special dinner tomorrow.'

'Why not?' said Richard, cheering up. He is always hungry.

'We'll invite Pauline and Peter and Joe and I shall cook—what shall I cook?'

'Trad roast beef and Yorkshire pud?'

'Beef's terribly expensive. What about chicken and lots of rice?'

'Yum yum.'

'Shall I ring Pauline or will you?'

'You ring her,' said Richard over-casually.

'And Richard,' I decided to strike while he was in a good mood. (Make people thoroughly uncomfortable for a few hours and they're so grateful when the discomfort stops that you can twiddle them round your little finger.)

'What?'

'When you get next term's grant do you think we could spend a little on home comforts?'

'Such as?'

'New lampshades and a salad bowl and glasses that match.'

'We might. What a little homebody you are, Emma.'

'I know. Is it bad, do you think?'

'You always want things settled and cosy and you hate change.'

'I know,' I said again, a little unhappily this time. I could visualise myself like Burns' mouse, continually making nests and having them torn up by the cruel plough.

'Put you in the middle of the Antarctic and you'd be spring cleaning your igloo and planning a new way of cooking whale blubber '

'But is it bad?'

'I think it could be,' said Richard seriously. 'Because

53

other people are adventurous and want to travel light. A musician for instance. Or an archaeologist.'

'Oh.'

Richard and I seldom had conversations like this for he had an uncanny knack of knowing what I was thinking and so we did not need to talk. But now I felt he was going to say something very important about my relationship with Alastair.

I wanted to hear it and then I decided I did not want to hear it at all.

'Everyone has to live somewhere,' I said defensively.

'According to an article I read musicians spend half their time in aeroplanes and the other half in hotel rooms.'

'A fat lot of composing you'd get done.'

'I could compose on the back of a laundry list in a waiting room at Crewe.'

'Then why were you making such a fuss about your working table?' I said smartly.

Richard grinned.

'You're quite right,' he said. But I still wondered what he had been going to say about me and Alastair. That the home-making glitter in my eye was frightening him off? That I wasn't gay and adventurous enough? And what, I wondered, was wrong between him and Pauline?

When I rang her she was delighted with the invitation but never mentioned his name at all.

'Can I bring anything?' she asked.

'You could bring some wine,' I suggested, for I wanted the dinner to be my own unaided work.

Peter and Joe were delighted too.

I bought a large boiling fowl, peppers and, very extravagantly, a quarter of mushrooms. I got chicory and a tin of pineapple for a salad and two different sorts of cheese. I had come to learn that having one splendid meal was better for one's morale than several indifferent ones. Richard and I would have to live on eggs and kippers and baked beans for the rest of the week but it would be worth it.

On Sunday morning I barricaded myself in the kitchen with all the ingredients laid out on the table and my favourite Elizabeth David cookery book. I chopped onions, peppers and uncooked ham and fried them gently in oil. I added the rice and when it had become golden and transparent I put it all into the biggest saucepan I could find. Then I carved the chicken, which I'd cooked the evening before. I wished I had a beautiful enamelled paella dish, a wooden salad bowl, plates that matched, streamlined cutlery with wooden handles, elegant wine glasses instead of tumblers. Perhaps I was an obsessive home-body. Perhaps I was unduly attached to possessions and the desire to have nice things. And I would end up in some ghastly overfurnished house with shutters to protect the curtains and newspapers to protect the carpet and antimacassars to protect the upholstery while Richard whisked round the world in an aeroplane and Alastair crouched in a tent in Egypt. It was a gloomy prospect. Sometime in the future I would have to psychoanalyse myself.

8

Everyone was very gay at lunch and I, resolutely banishing thoughts of Alastair, managed to be gay too. I had cleared the table in my room and we all sat round on chairs of varying heights, eating off plates of varying sizes and colours.

'Best meal I've had since I came to Edinburgh,' said Peter, beaming.

'You're a clever, clever poppet,' said Pauline.

'Quite a little mother to the others,' said Richard slyly and I kicked him under the table.

It was a nice feeling, to sit at the head of the table, dishing out delicious food to my friends.

'You create a home,' said Joe, whose English was not as good as Peter's, 'and that is very good. It is different upstairs. We are just two men with no woman to look after us. You are lucky, Richard, to have such a sister.'

It was a long speech for him and I blushed with pleasure. I would invite them more often, I decided. Some people at any rate appreciated my home-making qualities.

'Let us marry Emma and take her back to Nigeria with us,' said Peter. 'I believe men are being discouraged from having more than one wife but I do not see why a woman should not have two husbands. It will be progress.'

Over Alastair's dead body, I thought, but I responded to the joke, and said, 'A super idea.'

'We cannot let a jewel like Emma waste herself on one man,' Peter went on.

Just then I became aware of undercurrents of feeling flowing between Pauline and Richard. They had been very gay and non-committal with each other and now I was conscious that their relationship, which had always seemed to me so perfect and easy and affectionate, had a discordant element about it. Pauline defended polyandry vivaciously—and polygamy too—and she was very funny but Richard did not laugh.

'A hermit's life for me,' he said coolly.

'I'll find you a cave, darling,' said Pauline quickly, 'but are you sure you wouldn't like a little slave-girl to minister to your ego?'

'I don't know any slave girls,' said Richard.

I realised that they were talking about something quite different and it disturbed me.

'Can we try your new piece?' I asked him. 'Is it finished yet?'

'It's not finished but we might try,' said Richard.

So we went into his room; Peter fetched his guitar, Pauline assembled and tuned her oboe and I leaned over Richard's shoulder, at the piano, trying to decipher his black squiggly notes. I was not very reliable about sight reading but I had a good memory and after he had played my part on the piano a couple of times I thought I could hold it.

Peter was delighted with his part though Richard kept

ticking him off for improvising his own notes instead of following the manuscript.

'You play what I've written,' said Richard fiercely, 'none of your damned improvisations here.'

'But Richard, see, it is so much nice if I—'

'No.'

'Oh all right. You are a bloody dictator,' said Peter. 'I thought the British were democrats.'

Richard did become a dictator where music was concerned. He made us each perform alone before he allowed us to try it together. Since I was singing an unfamiliar part I could not really listen to the others at first, but gradually I became aware of the whole tapestry of sound, and as Richard had said the polyphonic form was Elizabethan but the harmonies were quite strange and modern.

'Where to should I express my inward heaviness?' I sang and the oboe circled round my voice, very plaintively, 'No mirth can make me fain, Till that we meet again.'

Joe sat by himself listening and he looked so sad that I thought 'Poor Joe, perhaps he has a girl in Nigeria and is missing her. Or perhaps he hasn't got one but would like to have one.'

'No!' shouted Richard suddenly. 'No, Pauline, B flat you idiot, not B natural.'

'It's your bloody writing,' said Pauline.

'It's as clear as day to anyone with an ear.'

'It's as clear as mud.'

'Go back to the double bar.'

The mood had been spoilt and soon I said that I was

tired (I was) and retired to my room. Joe followed me and we did the washing up together.

'Your brother is a funny boy,' he said.

'Why?'

'It is not what he says in words—but his music.'

'Oh.'

'He is very English or should I say Scottish, your brother.'

'Both actually. Our mother was Scottish.'

'His feelings only show in his music.'

This was true. I remembered the *In Memoriam* sonata he had written for mother and father which said in music all he felt about their tragic death, things he had never once put into words.

'That's because he's a composer,' I said, a little defensively.

'Not altogether,' said Joe. 'I think he would be happier if he could speak also.'

'Possibly,' I said, as lightly as I could.

'And you, Emma, are you happy?'

'I'm always happy,' I said quickly. In a way I would have liked to have a confidential conversation with Joe but I did not know him well enough.

He sighed and I at once felt guilty of repulsing him. I did hope he would not think it was because he was black.

'We all have problems, Joe,' I said at length.

'But you, Emma, are so pretty and charming and kind. And you are not black.'

'I might feel odd being white in Nigeria,' I said. I

couldn't stand him when he got into one of his self-pitying moods.

'No, everyone would love you as I do,' said Joe and I realised with relief that he was not going to give me a dissertation on race relations going back to, if not further than, the slave trade.

'Would you leave your girlfriend in order to go to a conference?' I suddenly asked him.

'A conference?' said Joe slowly. 'That would depend. But a conference with ideas I liked—I would expect her to come too, to share. The old style marriage, master and servant, no conversation, no sympathy, was bad. I like your new style, being equal. It is difficult but good.'

'Yes,' I said heavily, feeling depressed all over again. I thanked Joe for helping with the washing up and lay down on my bed. Surely everything—football, music, archaeology, politics, would take their proper place in our lives if we loved each other? And Alastair and I did love each other. He had said so.

I was just considering what to do next when there was a knock on my door and Pauline came in.

'I just came to thank you for my lovely lunch,' she said.

'It was a pleasure,' I said graciously.

Pauline wandered round my room and then suddenly burst out:

'Emma, Richard's impossible.'

'Impossible? In what way?'

'He treats me like a slave girl. Peter's quite right to describe him as a dictator.'

'But only about music surely?'

'Only about music,' Pauline spat out furiously. 'After

all, Emma, I'm a musician too and I don't see why I should agree with all his opinions and take orders from him on what to like and what to play and how to play it.'

She tossed her hair back defiantly. My heart sank. It mattered to me so much that they were happy together, even if it did make me a little envious at times.

'Have you told Richard how you feel?'

'Of course I have, but he just plays the maestro and won't listen. I do think he's fearfully talented—he may even be a genius—but all the same I don't want to spend every evening being ordered about.'

I pondered. Richard had always bullied me but that was because I was his younger sister and I did not mind. Besides he had always dashed to my rescue in times of crisis. But I could quite see that someone not his sister might resent his attitude. Still they did love each other and that should solve all their problems just as it would solve Alastair's and mine.

'Last weekend,' went on Pauline, 'I just about went mad because he wanted me to play some rotten Bartok and I don't like Bartok. And I wanted to go to the pub or have a meal out or go round to someone's house—you know, something sociable.'

'Oh dear,' I said sympathetically. (Bartok, football, there was always something.)

'So he told me I was adolescent and undisciplined and I told him he was a toffee-nosed old tyrant. And so on. That's why I stayed away all week. But I didn't really enjoy myself away from Richard.'

'He was pretty gloomy too,' I said helpfully.

Pauline wrapped her cloak around her with an exaggerated swirl and did a little pirouette.

'You know what I miss, Emma? Fun! We don't seem to have had any fun for ages. Not like we had on holiday.'

She brooded for a moment and then her face brightened.

'Emma, let's go out and walk the whole length of Princes Street and look into every single shop window. And then we'll have afternoon tea in a café with scones and gooey cream cakes. I don't care if I'm adolescent or not.'

'Let's!' I said. It was just what I felt like doing too. If I didn't look out I would be growing old before my time, weighed down by household cares and responsibilities. Feeling thoroughly female and frivolous I clattered down the stairs after Pauline.

When we returned, considerably refreshed, we bounced into Richard's room and Pauline tweaked his hair, kissed the tip of his nose and told him he was a medieval monster with a maestro complex.

'Emma and I have decided you're a genius but we're still not going to pander to your iron whims. Work is for weekdays but on Saturday and Sunday we shall be roystering and dissipated.'

'Women are frivolous creatures,' grumbled Richard, but he grinned as he said it, and seeing that they would be happily arguing for hours I tactfully withdrew.

9

Of course Alastair rang up the one evening I was out at choir practice. There was going to be a Christmas carol concert and we had started evening rehearsals. After the rehearsal John and several other people pressed me to go and have coffee and, remembering my resolution not to grow old before my time, I accepted. It was pleasant and undemanding to gossip with people of my own age whom I did not need particularly to impress with my cleverness or charm.

John behaved as if I were in his charge, offering to carry my music, to pay for my coffee and to give me a lift home, all of which I refused. But I did allow him to accompany me to the bus stop where we stood and talked. I enjoyed talking to him because he was really musical as well as having an excellent tenor voice. He told me that he had had a job singing in the chorus of the English Opera Company during the last Festival.

'It was marvellous,' he said.

'Which operas?'

'*Albert Herring, Figaro* and *The Barber of Seville*. It's completely different being inside an opera instead of outside.'

'But can you see the wood for the trees?'

'You can see the wood better after you've seen the trees in detail. Do you like opera?'

'I'm not sure. I haven't ever been to one. I've only listened to bits here and there on the radio.'

'Shall I take you when Sadlers Wells comes?'

'Mmm,' I said guardedly.

So it was after eleven when I got home, happily humming one of the carols under my breath, to find Richard brewing himself some coffee in the kitchen.

'Guess who phoned,' he said.

'Oh no, Richard,' I squeaked.

'Didn't you want him to?'

'Of course I did. But I wanted to be in. What did he say? When's he coming?'

'You are in a state,' reproved Richard. 'Calm down.'

'Don't be beastly. Tell me.'

'He's coming on Saturday: Waverley ten-thirty a.m.'

'Can he stay the night?'

'You mean on my sofa? I'll consider it.'

'You're marvellous. Everything's marvellous.'

To make things even better I got a letter from Aunt Patsy the next day enclosing two five pound notes.

'I had a bit of luck,' she wrote, 'and sold some illustrations to an American magazine, so here is a contribution towards your winter wardrobe. For goodness' sake get something warm and windproof—I know what Edinburgh winters are like. We're all counting the days to Christmas but are you sure Richard's car won't fall to pieces on the way? I'd be much happier to think of you on a train.'

64

Dear Aunt Patsy, I thought affectionately, getting quite an old fuss-pot in her old age. Of course Richard's car, held together, as he put it, with indiarubber bands and will-power, might easily break down. But then it easily mightn't. It was quite a sturdy, if ancient Rover, which got overheated going up hills and developed an alarming rattle if driven at more than forty miles an hour. Also the back doors wouldn't open from the outside and the front doors wouldn't open from the inside so we were always scrambling over seats to get into our appropriate places. Still, Richard said, the engine was magnificent and in some miraculous way the car had passed its M.O.T. test.

Now I had to get my winter coat. I rather hankered after a cloak like Pauline's but then I realised I wouldn't be able to wear it at school without Miss Smith having a thousand fits and being convinced I was taking drugs or trying my hand at housebreaking. So I reluctantly settled for a dark grey duffel coat lined with tartan and I thought I would ask Pauline to find a piece of fur in a junk shop to line the hood. This cost well under the ten pounds so I would have some extra money to buy nice things for Alastair at the weekend.

On Saturday morning I was dressed, breakfasted and out of the house the moment the shops opened, leaving an immaculate room behind me. I bought cheese, sliced sausage and salad for lunch and some fairly cheap steak for a stew on Sunday. I could pad it out with beans and vegetables—perhaps Alastair would help me chop up carrots and onions, or at least sit around and talk to me while I cooked. That only left Saturday supper and I decided eggs and bacon would do—there was always the chance that Alastair might have enough money to take me out.

I arrived, panting, at Waverley station at exactly ten twenty-five and stationed myself close to the barrier so that I would not lose one second of Alastair's company.

Railway stations are fascinating places. I always wonder who all these people can be, where they're going and why. Mum and Dad and two little boys going to visit Granny; a mysterious haughty girl with an expensive magazine going to meet her lover; fat men in dark suits with bulging briefcases off on business conferences; raucous youth on the way to some football match; middle-aged women with capacious shopping bags intending to visit Barrowland—the place in Glasgow, like Petticoat Lane—where you get fantastic bargains; and, in spite of the time of year, still the oddly conspicuous tourist with airline hold-alls and brightly labelled suitcases.

The train drew in and all these people, and dozens like them, streamed off the train, handing their tickets offhandedly at the barrier, some looking for familiar faces, some looking blindly ahead. But not one of them was Alastair.

When it became clear that the last passenger had gone I approached the ticket collector.

'That was the train from Glasgow, wasn't it?' I hazarded.

'Aye, aye.'

'And the next one?'

'Eleven o'clock.'

The ticket collector disappeared into his little box to

66

make mysterious calculations before he started letting more passengers through the barrier.

I was in despair and a thousand dreadful possibilities flashed through my mind. Alastair might be ill. Richard might have got the message wrong and it was next Saturday he meant. Alastair might have got involved in an accident on the way to the station. He might have changed his mind. He might be giving me the brush off.

I walked slowly into the buffet and ordered a coffee. I would wait for the next train and if he was not on that I would telephone Richard in case there was a message for me. It was curiously important not to ring Richard until after I had waited for the eleven o'clock train. It was not that Richard would crow, on the contrary I knew he would be sympathetic, but I did not want sympathy. It would be too humiliating.

I drank my horrible coffee slowly, looking at my watch after every second sip and staring vaguely and blindly at all these mysterious people who were waiting for trains, or, like me, for friends, relations and lovers coming off trains.

I made all sorts of bargains with fate. If five minutes had passed since I last looked at my watch; if I shut my eyes and counted to five hundred; if I waited to hear the announcer saying: 'The train now approaching platform twelve will be the ten o'clock from Glasgow Queen Street,' before I dashed out to meet it; if I could hold my breath for two minutes, then Alastair would be on the eleven o'clock.

At last I could bear it no longer and I walked out of the hot steamy buffet into the raw air. I went over to the bookstall and looked at the paperbacks.

I watched porters pulling enormous trolleys piled with luggage, mail bags and parcels; taxis disgorging passengers, people hurrying with that typically anxious, abstracted air that travellers have. And above the noise of traffic and trains there came the disembodied and distorted voice of the announcer—'the train now approaching ... the train now leaving ... passengers for ... and ... change at Carstairs, or Doncaster or Berwick....'

I stationed myself near the barrier and then I suddenly became panic stricken that perhaps this train would be coming in on a different platform. So I rushed up to a porter and asked him. He seemed to think I was a near mental defective but said crossly that of course it didn't. I relaxed.

The station clock now said eleven o'clock but it was always slightly fast. I shut my eyes and began to count.

At last, at long last the train drew in and yes, yes, there was Alastair in his shaggy jacket, grinning and waving.

I threw myself into his arms.

'Oh Alastair, I thought you were never coming.'

'I missed the train, idiot that I am. But it didn't seem worth while ringing up as you only had half-an-hour to wait.'

Only half-an-hour! It had seemed like half a year.

We walked up the steep hill out of the station, entwined and stopping several times to kiss.

'You're looking very smart, new coat?' asked Alastair.

'It's new but not smart. Aunt Patsy sent me some money. How was your conference?'

'Interesting. Mum has a sister in Belfast so we know

68

almost first hand how Catholics are treated.'

'You're not Catholics are you?' I asked, slightly alarmed as I did not want to find another difference between us.

'No, but I think everyone should have a square deal, don't you?'

'I certainly do,' I said fervently.

'Are you religious?'

'If there is a God I don't think he's particularly on my side,' I said, thinking of my parents' death. 'I think I just believe in fate.'

'You mean if a germ or a bomb has your name on it you'll catch it?'

'Roughly.'

'Is that comforting?'

'No, it's frightening. You feel so unsafe.'

We were struggling against the wind up Market Street and as we paused at the corner a gust nearly made me lose my balance. I gasped and clutched Alastair.

'See what I mean?'

We laughed.

'What do you believe in, Alastair?' I asked curiously. I realised I did not have the slightest idea.

'I believe that history makes a sort of pattern and if we're conscious of the pattern we can either help it or hinder it. I want to help it.'

'Even if you don't like the pattern?'

'But I do,' said Alastair. 'I think very gradually we're learning to use science and nature sensibly and to treat everyone as deserving certain basic rights but not unfair privileges.'

'What about pollution and radio-activity and these ghastly wars?'

'Some people always try to hold the clock back.'

Alastair and I had known each other such a short time, barely six months, and during that time we had mostly been apart, so we had not yet discovered the simplest things about each other. It was only a fortnight ago that I had discovered his interest in football. So all our conversations were extraordinarily exciting even if they made me nervous.

Now I had a sudden inspiration and as we reached—and were going to cross—the Royal Mile, I said:

'Come on to the Castle Esplanade and I'll show you the high house where I used to live with Aunt Patsy.'

'Where you tried to reform her?'

'Exactly.'

So we walked up the hill, the street paved with what they called granite setts, and on to the esplanade and then I showed Alastair the, let's face it, not very beautiful tenement, in the top floor of which I had spent two and a half years of my life.

'Jings,' said Alastair, 'how fabulous! I wish you lived there now.'

'So do I.'

He had passed some important test.

'What a view you must have had.'

'Oh yes, the Pentlands and the Castle and even the sea and the hills of Fife.'

'Lucky,' sighed Alastair. 'Tell me all about it.'

So I told him and it took us along George IV Bridge

and through the middle Meadow Walk towards March-mont.

'What's the programme?' he asked at last.

'I've bought food for lunch,' I said, 'and then I thought, oh we'd sit around—it's really up to you.'

'No party?'

'No party, but I daresay Richard and Pauline will be around.'

I had told Richard and Pauline that I would allow them to share our lunch but that I would not be responsible for their supper. Neither of them was in when we reached the flat, so Alastair and I had a pleasant hour together. One of the nice things about him was that he was sincerely interested in my school work and actually looked at and made helpful remarks about my history essays. Then we reminisced about our summer digging on the island and wondered whether we'd do it again this year. Alastair had a certain amount of field work to do for his degree but he had not made up his mind where he would do it.

'I've a great fancy to visit the Shetland islands and look at Jarlshof. I believe it's fantastic,' he said.

'Jarlshof?'

I ought to have known, but I didn't.

'There was a settlement there which is supposed to have lasted for about two thousand years before even the Norsemen came—a bronze-age village, a broch and a group of wheel-houses, all of different dates. Then the Vikings arrived but they weren't, apparently, the fierce warlike sort, just peasants and fishermen.'

'How do you know?'

'There haven't been any collections of weapons found of course, stupid.'

'What else?' I asked humbly.

'In the end and on top of all that Earl Patrick Stewart built himself a house there.'

'It does sound fascinating. But what about Mexico?'

'Too expensive,' said Alastair, practically. 'But in any case excavation has been so terribly neglected in Scotland that I'd like to be one of the people to redress the balance. I shall write the definitive book on the Bronze Age, as a start.'

'Yes, Professor Munro.'

He lectured me amiably about archaeology until Richard and Pauline arrived for lunch.

10

After lunch in Richard's room, we were sitting drinking coffee and the conversation naturally turned to Christmas and Richard's car.

'Ah yes, the famous car,' said Alastair. 'Will it hold out?'

'It's in rather poor health at the moment,' said Richard gloomily. 'Indigestion, heart condition, something.'

'Perhaps it needs psycho-analysing,' suggested Pauline.

'Do you know anything about cars, Alastair?' Richard asked.

'A bit,' said Alastair modestly and then to my horror they went into a long involved conversation about jets, inner and outer bearings, float chambers, pistons and sparking plugs. To me a car is just a method of getting from A to B and I've never been able to understand how some people can spend hours and hours studying models they haven't a hope of buying, comparing horse powers, front wheel and back wheel drives, and acceleration power and so forth.

'I'll take a look at it, if you like,' offered Alastair at length and the two boys went out together, without even a word of apology to Pauline and myself.

We stared at each other blankly; then the humour of the situation struck us at the same moment and we burst into giggles.

'Men!' we spluttered.

'Let's watch them out of the window,' said Pauline and we leaned out. There they were, heads bent over the wretched car's insides. They were prodding something, Richard fetched a screwdriver, Alastair rubbed something with an oily rag, Richard got in and started the engine, Alastair peered into the bonnet with an absorbed expression.

'Grrr, it's cold,' I said, shutting the window.

'There's a good afternoon disappeared,' said Pauline. 'Well, I've got some shopping to do. Want to come?'

'N-no, I'd better not.'

'Come on, Emma, don't be a doormat.'

'I'll clear up and cook the stew for tomorrow.'

'If you've any sense you'll leave them to do the clearing up. And cook their own wretched stew.'

'What shall I tell Richard?'

'Nothing at all. If he wants me he can jolly well find me.'

She left me and slowly and very gloomily I washed up the lunch things and prepared my stew. So I had been foolish enough to imagine Alastair helping me, or at any rate sitting companionably beside me chatting! Not all the tears in my eyes were due to the onions.

The boys came clattering cheerfully up the stairs about an hour later, still talking about jets and sparking plugs, and highly delighted with themselves.

'She's bounding about like a two-year-old now,' said

Richard with satisfaction.

'Ugh,' I said.

'Where's Pauline?'

'Out.'

'I'll just have a wash,' said Alastair, going whistling into the bathroom.

'What's the matter? Did I steal your boyfriend?' asked Richard offensively.

'Oh shut up!' I barked, going into my room and slamming the door.

Presently Alastair re-appeared, dragging a comb through his mane, his face pink and shiny from the rough towel.

'What shall we do now?' he asked brightly.

'I don't know.'

'Walk? Cinema?'

'Don't care.'

'Emma! What's the matter? You're not annoyed with me, are you? Because I helped Richard with the car?'

'Do what you like. It's all one to me.'

'But we need the car for going to Oban at Christmas.'

I made an indeterminate sound, half sob, half grunt. Speech was quite beyond me. I turned my back on Alastair and stared out of the window, fighting back tears.

He came up behind me and put his arms round me.

'Emma,' he said, 'darling Emma, don't.'

I turned round and burrowed into his pullover, which I hoped would muffle my sobs.

Eventually I allowed him to soothe me, to kiss away my tears, to tell me that he couldn't bear me to be unhappy, to say that I was sweet and foolish.

I was warm and happy and comforted but at the same time bitterly ashamed. For I knew I had done something terribly wrong and that the number of times a girl can get her own way by bursting into tears is strictly limited.

II

We were very quiet and tender with each other for the rest of the evening. First we went out, for Alastair had not often been to Edinburgh and wanted to explore the Royal Mile. So we sauntered slowly down and examined all the wynds and closes, the houses that were falling to pieces and the ones that had been beautifully renovated. Alastair was as fascinated as I had been so that by the time we reached the Canongate and Holyrood Palace, it was almost dark. So we took a bus back up and Alastair offered to buy me a Chinese meal. After my experience at the cinema I did not dare to offer to pay my share, but I let Alastair choose for me so that I should not pick on anything too expensive. It was a delicious meal and afterwards we lingered over green tea in little handle-less cups, holding hands and feeling very lover-like.

At last Alastair asked for the bill and I dashed to the Ladies' cloakroom so that I wouldn't see it and feel embarrassed. Then, arm in arm we stepped into the street. Alastair looked at his watch.

'I think I'll catch the ten o'clock,' he said. 'Will you walk down to the station with me, or are you tired?'

I couldn't believe it and for a moment I was utterly speechless.

'B-but I thought you were going to stay the night,' I stammered.

'Sorry, love. I've got a meeting tomorrow morning I must be back for.'

'But, Alastair, you said—' and then I remembered, it was Richard who had given me the message. I would skin him alive when I got home. And then I remembered again. I had asked if Alastair could stay the night and Richard had offered his sofa. I'd simply taken it for granted that he would. But this did not lessen my disappointment.

'Richard gave me the wrong message,' I mumbled. 'Couldn't you possibly stay?'

'Sorry,' repeated Alastair, I thought rather sharply.

I hated him bitterly and I knew I would either burst into tears again or lose my temper. But I simply must not burst into tears. I must stop being a doormat.

'I think you're rotten,' I burst out, 'you never have time.'

'Emma!'

'There's always a meeting or a football match or a car —or something.'

'Emma, for goodness sake,' and he really sounded cross now.

We were standing on the corner of the street and I was making an exhibition of myself, I knew, and yet I couldn't stop.

We glared at each other. Then Alastair said in a low cold voice:

'I'm sorry that's the way you feel,' and walked away. I gazed after him in agony, wanting to scream. But I didn't. With my head down, blinking back my tears, I crossed the road and prepared to go home up the Middle Meadow Walk. I was halfway along when panic hit me. I couldn't let Alastair go. I looked at my watch. It was quarter to ten and if I ran all the way I might just get to Waverley before the train departed.

I ran and ran, gasping his name, nearly knocking people over, darting between cars, and just as I pelted down the steep incline into the station I saw his unmistakeable figure halfway down.

'Alastair!' I called, with my last breath.

He turned and I panted up to him, seizing his hand.

'Alastair, I'm sorry. I'm terribly sorry. I was just so disappointed. I didn't mean what I said.'

So he missed the train and we stood together near the platform entrance while I apologised all over again.

'Emma, you mustn't get into such states. You make me feel—so responsible.'

'I won't again. I promise.'

'I want you to be happy.'

'I'm only happy with you.'

'But you mustn't only be happy with me. That's exactly what I mean.'

'I don't understand.'

'Nobody can be responsible for someone else's happiness.'

'I see,' I said limply.

'Now cheer up, love, and I'll be in touch soon.'

I wanted to ask 'When?' but I bit the question back.

'Lovely,' I said, with false brightness.

He kissed me goodbye, but with a kind brotherly kiss

79

instead of the passionate one I wanted. I waved and forced myself to smile.

I walked slowly home. I was completely fagged out. If I'd had the money I would have taken a taxi and yet I needed some time by myself to try and sort out my feelings.

I was disgusted with myself for sobbing and screaming, being possessive and tiresome, resenting everything that took Alastair away from me. No wonder he was fed up with me.

'You've got to turn over a new leaf and pretty smartly too,' I told myself sternly.

And yet I still felt that Alastair was unfairly neglectful. How insecure and vulnerable I had become since I fell in love.

Once again I was in the Middle Meadow walk, the broad tree-lined path across the green open space where boys play football and people exercise their dogs and their children. Beneath every leafless tree and as far away from the golden lamplight as they could get, couples were standing, motionless and intertwined, mouth to mouth, neither moving nor speaking though sometimes I could see a hand tightening at the back of his or her neck. I was envious with a heartaching envy. How I longed to be one of two people united in this inseparable way! Oh Alastair, Alastair!

12

By now John had fallen noticeably in love with me. He used to hang about outside the school waiting for me to arrive in the morning and he contrived to run into me accidentally at least five times a day. If I went to the shop across the road to buy bridies or cheese rolls he was always there too, buying chocolate or lemonade for me without being asked, while the sixth-year girls, who considered him as their property, fumed with jealousy.

The trouble was that since he had fallen in love he had become shyer and less talkative. He would blush and fidget nervously while he wracked his brains for something startling to say, and cast imploring looks in my direction. Frequently I had to come to his rescue and remark how cold it was, ask him his opinion on the choir's progress and if he had been to any good concerts lately.

Still he was the nearest approach to a friend that I had got and this Monday, when once again he ventured to offer me a lift home on the back of his scooter, I was feeling so depressed over my disastrous Saturday with Alastair that I weakly accepted. It was rather splendid to whirl away through the traffic instead of queueing obediently at the bus stop.

When we reached home I thanked him warmly and this encouraged him to ask me to go to a concert with him.

'Please come with me, Emma.'

'Well, I don't know—' I began.

'I know you have a boyfriend in Glasgow,' he said, looking down at his feet, 'but surely we could be friends. I think—' he gulped, 'you're marvellous. If I could just see you sometimes.'

In spite of myself I couldn't help feeling flattered. Admiration is very soothing.

'What are they playing?' I asked, so that he would realise it was the music I was interested in and not his company.

'Mozart, Vaughan Williams a-and Prokofiev. Listen, do you have to go in now? Couldn't you come for a coffee?'

I considered. After all John was nice and it wouldn't hurt me to be kind to him as long as he knew that my affections were irrevocably fixed elsewhere.

'I'll make you a cup of coffee if you like,' I said at length. 'Come on in.'

So he parked his scooter and followed me into the house.

Everything, according to John, was marvellous. The fact that I lived with my brother, my Nigerian divan cover, my orange curtains, the expert way I made coffee, my collection of books. He positively glowed with appreciation.

He asked me what Richard did and when I told him he was a composer I thought he'd fall off his chair with excitement.

'Do you think,' he spluttered, 'that I could ever hear any of his work?'

'I don't see why not,' I replied graciously. 'Richard loves showing off. If he comes in soon you can ask him.'

He told me that he wanted to study music himself and possibly become an opera singer but his family were dead against it. 'They don't think singing is work,' he said, 'they think I ought to work in a bank. What do you want to do, Emma?'

'First I want to go to university and study history and archaeology or perhaps anthropology.'

'How marvellous. Most girls don't want to do anything much, do they?'

'Oh, I wouldn't say that.'

'They just want to get married. Do you want to get married, Emma?'

I winced. Of course I wanted to get married. But the prospect at the moment did not seem particularly rosy.

'Oh, eventually,' I said airily, 'but I think student marriages are a mistake.'

I was thinking longingly of living with Alastair in some flat I didn't care where, dashing home gaily in between lectures to laugh and kiss and talk, doing the weekend shopping together, inviting friends in for coffee and cheap but imaginative meals, helping each other over exams, decorating and making shelves, having Aunt Patsy and Stephen to stay, planning holidays.... But marriage had obviously never entered Alastair's head.

'They often are,' agreed John, 'but I suppose it depends on the people and whether you have any money or not. I won't have any money for years and years—if ever.'

'Neither will I.'

Just then I heard Richard come in so I opened my door and introduced John to him.

'John would like to hear you play,' I added.

'If it wouldn't be too much trouble,' mumbled John.

'No trouble at all,' said Richard. 'Just wait until I've warmed up. Now what shall I play?'

'Something—one of your own compositions.'

'I've been working on a group of three nocturnes so I'll give them an airing.' Richard said, sitting down at the piano. 'Can you read music? You can follow the score if you like.'

John accepted the manuscript as if he'd been offered a rare first edition and sat, hardly daring to breathe, while Richard began to play.

I did not particularly care for these nocturnes. I expected nocturnes to be dreamy and romantic like Chopin's but Richard was now so scornful of his 'juvenile lyricism' that he avoided any suggestion of sustained melody. But John was ecstatic.

'Marvellous,' he repeated. 'Please go on.'

When Richard had played all three nocturnes and a very fast noisy toccata he said pleasantly:

'Now I'm afraid I must throw you out. I have to work.'

John blushed scarlet, jumped to his feet and began apologising. I felt so sorry for him I almost asked him to stay to supper but I felt I'd heard the word 'marvellous' enough for one evening.

'So must I,' I said.

84

'I'm terribly sorry, I didn't mean to stay so long. But it's so seldom I meet anyone who really knows about music.' He stumbled out of the room after me. 'Your brother's fantastic, Emma, fantastic.'

'I think the toccata's hideous,' I snapped.

'You can't mean it.'

'I do. It's just a show-off piece. He's written some much better things.'

'Well, you probably know more about it than I do,' John said meekly. 'It must be marvellous to live here, on your own, like this.'

'It's jolly hard work.'

'But having no parents around to nag you. I bet you're a marvellous cook too.'

'I'm fair.'

I was feeling quite saturated with compliments so to speed his departure I handed him his scarf. As he took it I knew he wanted to kiss me.

'Emma,' he began.

'Goodbye,' I said quickly, 'see you tomorrow.'

'Goodbye and thank you. Please let me come again some time.'

I smiled graciously feeling like a queen dismissing a faithful knight, a little ridiculous in fact. It was curious, I thought, that I wanted Alastair to think me marvellous and he clearly didn't while John did and I faintly despised him for it. Nevertheless I did feel slightly less depressed. I couldn't be quite so dumb and plain and stupid and boring as I had thought. I decided to write to Alastair while my morale was high.

'Darling Alastair,' I wrote. That was always easy. And

then came doubts. Should I apologise for my stupid behaviour? Should I tell him about John in the hope of making him jealous? Oh, if only I could tell him spontaneously everything I thought and felt, instead of having to apply such rigorous censorship! For once, I would try.

'Darling Alastair,

I felt dreadful after you had gone. How stupidly and embarrassingly I had behaved. But you see I had misunderstood Richard's message and had been counting on spending Sunday with you too. We meet so seldom that when we are together I'm conscious all the time of how soon we have to part. And this makes me edgy and nervous and resentful of all the things you do and people you see away from me. I'm not really resentful, basically, I mean. And if I saw you more often I would be quite content to share you with football and motor cars and conferences. But I do love you, darling Alastair, and there is a curious lack of flavour about my life without you. This boy John who brought me home from school today on his scooter; he's very nice and musical and polite but oh how boring he is. (He thinks I'm marvellous by the way.) I hope you will come again soon and I promise to behave sensibly. Or I will come to Glasgow. And then let us have an absolutely gorgeous Christmas together on the island. Oh I can't wait. Write or ring soon and take thousands of kisses from,

your Emma.'

I read the letter through and tore it up into small pieces. Then I took a new sheet of paper and wrote:

'Darling Alastair,

'I don't know what came over me on Saturday evening —but you know about red-heads and their vile tempers. An adoring swain has just been up for coffee and music, though whether it was my beautiful eyes or Richard's beautiful music that brought him up, I'm not quite sure. He just murmurs MARVELLOUS from time to time. What about next weekend? Glasgow? Edinburgh? Do phone, but not on Friday as I'm going to a concert. Love Emma.'

I thought this was a gay casual affectionate letter which should go far to efface the image of the squawling tear-stained Emma he had last seen.

I began to day dream—first of all about Christmas. Sometimes the weather was quite mild, even in winter, and if so we would climb the highest hill on the island and look at the snowy peaks on the mainland, which always looked so delectable and mysterious. We would visit the nature conservancy and watch the deer and study rock formations. And in the evenings we would all sit round the peat fire and talk and play music. Everyone would be gay and unselfconscious; we'd decorate the Christmas tree and give each other small presents and fill Vanessa's stocking.

Then my thoughts wandered farther ahead to when I too would be a student and we'd spend our vacations together and have a life of travel and adventure, collaborating perhaps on a book about prehistoric remains in Scotland.

'Hey,' called Richard, coming into my room, 'what's for supper? I'm starving.'

I looked at him with a glazed stare, still a hundred miles away.

'What?'

'Supper.'

'Oh supper. There's some stew left—I'll pad it out with a can of beans.'

'Well don't moon, concentrate. Your first job is to feed me.'

'It's high time you learnt to feed yourself. I shall give you cooking lessons.'

'Ha, ha,' snarled Richard, going back into his room.

My train of thought was broken. All I could think of now was how soon Alastair would reply to my letter, when he would ring up, if I would see him this weekend.

13

Alastair did not write or phone all week and by Friday I was feeling sick with worry and dread. And John's attentions and solicitude seemed to me particularly annoying. 'I am looking forward to Friday,' he kept saying and it took a real effort on my part to force my lips into a smile. 'I'll call for you just after seven,' John insisted.

'It's perfectly all right. I'll meet you in the foyer.'

'No, I'll call for you.'

I knew he was dying to be asked round earlier but I could not bring myself to frame the invitation.

'Oh all right,' I said ungraciously.

'What's the matter?' Richard asked me as I banged bad-temperedly round the kitchen.

'John's such a moron,' I grumbled.

'He's not a moron at all. He's just love-sick. And love, my dear Emma, makes morons of us all.'

'Pah!' I retorted.

I stumped into my room to change, though what was the use of making myself look pretty for John, when he would probably think I looked marvellous if I turned up wearing sack-cloth. Still, I put on my dark green jersey frock and the copper medallion that Stephen had given me for my birthday, checked my tights for snags, brushed my hair and mascara-ed my eyelashes. It was another contrariwise fact of life that often when I cared least I looked my best. Although I was worried and unhappy and going out with a boy I didn't care two hoots about I looked elegant and glowing. It was most unfair. Still, at least I wasn't hungry and it gave me a little bitter satisfaction to put Richard's supper on the table saying nonchalantly, 'I don't want any.'

'Dieting?' asked Richard, cocking an eyebrow.

'No,' I snapped, 'just not hungry.'

'Wonders will never cease.'

'Oh shut up.'

Richard met my eyes and he said in a different gentle tone of voice.

'Ten years from now, five years from now, you'll hardly remember. It's just now that's difficult.'

So he did know how I was feeling. I smiled wanly but gratefully.

Then the doorbell rang and seizing my coat I ran downstairs to meet John. As I expected he said:

'Emma, you look marvellous.'

'Thank you.'

I really did enjoy the concert in a macabre sort of way. I didn't so much listen to the music but allowed it to wash over me while I brooded over the unhappiness of my life.

How few had been the moments of accord and happiness in the four months I had known Alastair. I remembered our evenings on the island, walking slowly through the darkened landscape, listening to the sea and standing on the little bridge to kiss goodnight. And I remembered how glad I'd been at the prospect of coming back to Edinburgh because it would be so easy to see Alastair at weekends. And it hadn't been easy at all and when we had met things had gone wrong so that instead of glowing memories I only had a sense of dissatisfaction and regret. Was it because of my nasty possessive character or because Alastair was cooling off? Or were we—what was the word—incompatible? No, that was a possibility I refused to face. All that we needed was more time together. I was so deeply embedded in my painful thoughts that when the concert ended I looked at John almost with surprise, as if to saw what are *you* doing here? He smiled at me, a shy wistful smile and I wondered what he had been thinking about, perhaps he had been weaving day dreams too and wishing they would come true.

'Do you want to go straight home or will you come and have a coffee with me?' he asked.

'Home,' I said wearily.

'Oh Emma, please.'

I pulled myself together.

'O.K. I was forgetting it was Friday.'

He beamed gratefully and, putting his hand under my elbow, guided me through the crowds.

'The Mozart was too slow, didn't you think?' he asked.

'Mm.'

'It made it sentimental and Mozart's never sentimental.'

'No.'

He opened the door of a snack bar, all nicely done up in pitch-pine panelling, full of smoke and steam and cooking smells.

'Have a cake or a sandwich or a hamburger?'

I considered. After all I was unhappy and oughtn't to to be hungry, but my sometimes overwhelming housekeeping duties made me find food I had not bought or cooked myself, and which I wouldn't have to wash up afterwards, almost irresistible.

'Hamburger would be nice,' I murmured.

'Just what I feel like too.'

We sat down with coffee and hamburgers and John solicitously pressed pepper, salt, mustard and sugar towards me.

'I hope you don't mind me asking,' he said, 'and just slap me down if you do mind, but are your parents divorced or something?'

'No, they died when I was thirteen, in a car crash.'

'Oh gosh, I am sorry.'

'It's all right. My aunt adopted me.'

So I told him about Aunt Patsy and Stephen and Vanessa and the island and in a way I liked telling him.

'My parents are going to be divorced,' he said jerkily, when I'd finished. 'I thought you might be in the same boat and we could talk about it together.'

For the first time I suddenly realised that John was a person with his own problems, and not just a love-sick swain whose attentions I was prepared to put up with.

'We could still talk about it,' I said. 'What happened?'

'My father left home. I think he must have fallen in love with someone else. Then he came back and there were awful conversations, you know, the sort that break off every time you enter the room. Now he's gone again and mother told me he wasn't coming back this time.'

'Is she terribly upset?'

'Terribly. She goes on and on about having wasted the best years of her life and what selfish beasts men are.' He paused and then, in a rush: 'She's drawn all the money out of the joint bank account and bought a new carpet.'

I could tell that John wanted me to approve, or at least understand, but I was horrified. 'But that's awful,' burst from me before I had time to think.

'She says he would have done the same thing if she hadn't got in first?'

'And would he?'

'I don't know.'

To me the thought that people, after living together for twenty years, could be so cruel and revengeful, was beyond my comprehension. I had always imagined that people tried to be kind to each other even if they did not always succeed. There must have been some sort of warfare going on, of which surely John must have been conscious.

'Didn't your father talk to you?' I asked.

'He never said a word.'

'Were they happy together—before?'

'I thought so. They never talked much, just the sort of "Had a good day at the office, dear" conversation, but they didn't quarrel.'

'Perhaps he got bored.'

'Obviously,' said John bitterly. 'So now you see why I'll have to go into a bank and not be a singer because

I'll never be able to leave Mother.'

'She may find someone else, too.'

'You don't know my mother. Now I know what it means about the sins of the father being visited on the sons.'

'Do you hate him?'

'Yes, I think I do.'

'I'm sure marriage is really very difficult,' I said slowly, 'I don't think you should blame anyone particularly. I think you should talk to your father and try to see his point of view.'

'I never want to see him again,' John said. 'He's ruined my mother's life.'

Curiously, instead of joining in an 'all men are beasts' session, I found myself defending John's father. I could just imagine his mother, small and mousy and pathetic, nagging him about bringing mud into the kitchen and never talking about anything except the price of food or the unmannerly behaviour of the neighbours' children.

And now, doubtless, she would make John's life a misery, wanting to know where he was going and why and who with, and telling him that now he was all she'd got and that he ought to be grateful for all the sacrifices she had made for him.

So I said belligerently:

'I don't see why she talks of wasting the best years of her life. She was married for twenty years and had you. How can experience be waste?'

'But it's too late for her to marry again, she's lonely and unhappy and it's all Dad's fault.'

'Nothing is ever one person's fault,' I said wisely, 'and in any case'—I suddenly saw the whole thing very clearly —'you have to be happy in yourself because of who you are and what you do, not because of someone else. Being responsible for someone's happiness is like being in prison.'

Of course! That was what Alastair had been trying to tell me. I, with my demands, had been offering him nothing but a bright cosy prison.

'I never thought you would be so cool and hard,' John said, puzzled.

'But John, don't you see, it isn't strong people who are tyrants, it's weak ones, people who are dependant. Like ivy. It climbs over a stone wall and pulls out the stones, and it climbs up a tree and strangles it.'

'Are you suggesting that my mother is like ivy?'

'I don't know her,' I said flatly.

'Well let me tell you that she isn't like that at all. She's very brave and kind and after all she is my responsibility—now. I'll have to go into that bank—but it isn't because she's asked me to. It's because I feel I must.'

'I'm sure she won't want you to, if you really want to study music. There are scholarships and things.'

'Scholarships aren't the same as bringing money into the house,' said John gloomily.

I felt really sorry for him. At the same time I wanted so much to see Alastair again, to tell him what I had learned, and that I completely understood his behaviour, that I could hardly wait.

'I must go,' I said.

'O.K.'

A letter would take so long; a telephone was impossible. Suddenly I decided I'd go into Glasgow tomorrow without an invitation.

In the meantime, feeling that I had been rather priggish and superior to poor John, I explained:

'I'm only speaking out of the top of my head. If it were my own mother I'm sure I'd feel exactly like you do.'

14

When I arrived at Queen Street station the following morning I was suddenly torn with doubt. With no Alastair to meet me I felt desolate and lonely amid all these scurrying, purposeful people. I decided to make a sentimental pilgrimage to the same café to brood over my plan of campaign. Perhaps it was a café where Alastair often went. There was possibly a million to one chance that he might be there. Although I knew how unlikely it was I could not help feverishly scanning the occupants of the tables before I sat down by myself and ordered coffee.

The thing was, should I be very bright and casual and pretend I had come to Glasgow for a quite different reason, but what? To visit friends? But I had no friends in Glasgow. The dentist? But obviously my dentist would be in Edinburgh. To go to a concert? Unlikely. To go to the Art Gallery? Yes, that was just possible. But would I be able to carry it off?

Or should I simply admit that I wanted to see him to clear up misunderstandings?

It struck me with dreadful clarity that our relationship must be a pretty poor one if I could not be direct and sincere with him. If he didn't like me as I truly was it would be better to break the whole thing off. I gulped the rest of my coffee and hurried out to find a bus.

But when I reached the scheme of new flats my courage deserted me and I walked up and down, eyeing the windows of Alastair's flat and wondering if he were in and, if he were, how he would react to my unannounced visit. Men did not like being hunted down by over-eager girlfriends. If he had wanted me to come he would have phoned or written. On the other hand, he did not know my revelation of truth about possessiveness being tyranny and how I had turned over a new leaf.

I started some of my acts of propitiating fate by counting with eyes shut, walking round the paved quadrangle without treading on the lines and so on.

And then Alastair appeared. He was bareheaded and fur-jacketed, whistling and looking so gay and normal that my heart thumped.

'Alastair!' I called.

'Emma!'

He was over to me in a few quick strides and then his arms were round me and he was kissing me, thoroughly and enthusiastically.

'Emma, you never said you were coming.'

'It was a sudden impulse.'

'You must have more of them.'

We laughed happily together.

'I have to go to the library,' said Alastair, 'but we'll have a coffee first.'

I put my arm through his and we walked to the bus stop. I felt like singing. All my worries and doubts and soul-searching seemed utterly stupid now. Although it was a damp grey foggy day, for me the sun was shining and all the shopping crowds seemed gay and festive. The bus conductor was jolly, mothers were affectionate to their children, young couples looked as if they were in love, old people as if they were wise and philosophic— I liked them all.

'Thanks for your letter, by the way. Sorry I haven't had time to answer it.'

'Work?'

'Partly. And I'm on the committee for this Civil Liberties campaign.'

'Oh,' I said.

'What have you been doing?'

'I went to a concert last night. And we've been rehearsing for our carol service.'

I couldn't talk to him seriously on the bus. I would wait until we were in the café, but the café, near the university library, was unfortunately full of Alastair's friends. They greeted him. He introduced me and before I had had a chance to say anything that was on my mind, we were in the middle of jokes about who had been doing what last night, who had failed or was about to fail his exams, the deplorable character of some professor or other, and general student gossip. Alastair did try to bring me into the conversation but when he explained that I came from Edinburgh all his friends did was to make the old stale jokes about Edinburgh being 'east windy and west-endy'. Just to make me feel at home, I thought bitterly.

Although I had only lived in Edinburgh for a short time I already felt strongly proprietorial about it. I loved the spiky sky-line of the city, and the folds of the Pentland Hills—now striped with snow—and the sudden views of the sparkling sea and the green trees in Princess Street gardens.

'But Edinburgh is at any rate beautiful,' I burst out.

'It's people that count,' said someone.

'At any rate we don't spend our time baiting Glaswegians,' I retorted.

'What about the haar,' sneered someone else.

Haar is a special Edinburgh sea mist that creeps in from the sea, very white and thick and damp but bearing no relation to fog or smog. Sometimes it can make high buildings like the Castle look very strange and dramatic, and the trees in the Meadows look as if they were floating on a white sea.

'Better than your smog,' I muttered.

Alastair nudged me.

'I think Edinburgh's beautiful,' he said, smiling.

While this conversation was taking place I began studying Alastair's friends, especially the female ones. Joan was a little mouselike creature, with light brown hair and freckles, who sat silently smiling little secret smiles to herself. I decided she would be unlikely to appeal to Alastair but Susan presented a far greater challenge. She had longish straight dark hair, parted in the middle, and one of those clear brown skins that glow with health. Her grey eyes were set wide apart under beautifully arched eye-brows and she smoked gracefully and confidently. She did not appear to be attached to any of the men in the group and I could not help wondering if she had expected to meet Alastair without me.

'I've done those posters,' she told him, 'or rather I got a tame art student to do them. How many do you want?'

'About half a dozen, I should think,' said Alastair. 'They're for a meeting we're holding next week,' he explained to me, 'we've got a Greek and a South African, who've both been political prisoners, as speakers.'

'You should come through for it,' said Susan kindly to me. 'Well, I must catch the library before it closes.'

'So must I,' said Alastair, treacherously. 'Come on, Emma.'

So we all three walked to the library together.

'What are you studying?' I asked Susan, feeling sure it would be something very esoteric and I was right, it was bio-chemistry.

However it did mean that she had to go to a different bit of the library.

'Will you come and collect the posters some time?' she asked Alastair.

'I'll give you a ring,' said Alastair.

'Cheerio then, bye Emma.' She smiled at us both and disappeared.

'She's a great girl,' Alastair murmured tactlessly. 'She was top of the whole second year.'

I gulped.

'She's awfully good-looking,' I said.

'I suppose she is,' Alastair said carelessly.

'Has she got a boyfriend?'

'Dozens I expect but I think she's pretty involved in her work.'

While Alastair found his books I stood idly, sniffing

in the leather library smells and envying Susan deeply. How splendid to be a beautiful clever bio-chemist! When Alastair returned I wanted badly to ask him if she was a special friend or just one of the gang but I did not dare.

'Now,' he said, 'what's the programme? Shall we go back to my place? Mum won't have cooked a special dinner but I daresay she'll rustle up a sandwich.'

'What would you be doing if I wasn't here?'

'I'd probably have a pint and pie in the pub.'

'Then let's do that.'

'Then I shall fall foul of the law by buying intoxicating liquor for an under-eighteen.'

'I'll have ginger beer.'

The pub was, thank goodness, not full of Alastair's friends and we sat down at a table in comparative privacy.

'I wanted to talk to you,' I said at last.

'About something special?'

'To explain really.'

A flicker crossed Alastair's face—was it impatience? I couldn't be sure.

'You don't have to,' he said quickly. 'You take everything so seriously, Emma.'

'But shouldn't I?'

'Not if it makes you unhappy.'

He took a swallow of beer, wiped his mouth with the back of his hand and smiled at me affectionately, yet somehow evasively.

'But I wanted you to know that I do understand what you said about people having to be happy on their own and not being possessive.'

'Of course.'

'I never will be again. It's just that I see you so seldom.' In spite of my resolution, my voice quivered.

'I know. It's hellish,' said Alastair. 'But, Emma, you're so very young. You must get about, meet people, do things. I'd be a monster if I—let our feelings for each other—restrict your life. I can't help feeling responsible.'

'But you're not,' I lied quickly. 'You're not responsible for me at all.' And then I asked that fatal question which no one should ever ask. 'But you do still love me, don't you?'

Again that flicker came on Alastair's face.

'Of course,' he said quickly. 'Now, Emma, no more soul-searching. Would you like to go to the pictures?'

'What had you planned to do?'

'Nothing much. I've got some notes to copy out but I can do that tomorrow.'

'Then I'd love to go to the pictures.'

Oh the bliss of sitting in the warm scented darkness, with my head on Alastair's shoulder and my hand holding his! And yet I could not get rid of the suspicion that things were not as right as they seemed. I went over the conversation in my head, trying to remember exactly what each of us had said. He did not want to be responsible for my happiness—that was clear—and of course he was quite right. But should a lover be quite so sensible and clear-headed about such a thing? Did he still see me as a pet lamb, nice to cuddle but often rather a nuisance?

'What would you like to do now?' Alastair asked as we came out of the cinema. He looked quickly, and surreptitiously, at his watch and I had a definite feeling that he had other plans for the evening which he would alter for my sake, but a little unwillingly.

To hell with sincerity and truthfulness.

I looked at my own watch and gave a gasp of astonishment.

'Gosh is it as late as that? I must find a train. We're having a musical evening and I'm needed. Richard's been composing some things with a vocal part. He wants me to learn the flute, actually, but I don't have time at present. My voice isn't really strong enough but I daresay John will fill in.'

'John?'

'A boy at school. The one who took me to the concert last night—he has a fabulous tenor voice.'

'Then I'll take you to the station,' said Alastair, but I could not tell from his voice what he was thinking.

I chattered desperately about our music, sounding as knowledgeable as possible and casually throwing in words like 'polyphonic' and 'contrapuntal'.

Luckily there was a train within five minutes of our arrival at the station for I was running out of words, my mouth was dry and my lips had begun to twitch and tremble. I was just able to gasp:

'Goodbye. I must run. I've had a lovely time.'

'Goodbye, Emma. See you soon. I'll be in touch.'

We kissed briefly and then I turned away and ran up the platform to the front of the train. I had behaved impeccably and Alastair would never know that now the tears were streaming down my cheeks.

15

I sat slumped in sodden despair, seeing and hearing nothing. I did not even notice when the train eased away from the platform and hooted before it went into the tunnel. But my fellow-travellers soon intruded into my gloomy thoughts. Probably they were just the same sort of people who had appeared so charming on the Glasgow bus, but now I saw them through different eyes. I saw a pompous sleekly-dressed young man with a thin cruel mouth; two blowsy girls giggling over a magazine, a middle-aged couple obviously bored with being married to each other.

Opposite me sat a grey soggy man, studying the racing results in his evening paper and I noticed with horror and repulsion that he kept dropping the top layer of his false teeth over his lip and then clicking it back into position. Beside him was a harassed mother with two whining children.

'Can I have some sweeties, Mum?'

'Mum, I'm thirsty, can I have some lemonade?' they repeated in an endless duet.

'No, you can't,' snapped the mother. 'Sit quiet and behave yoursels.'

'Want some crisps.'

'Want some sweeties.'

'You'll make yoursels sick if you have any more,' said the mother, weakly taking a bag of sweets out of a hold-all. 'I'll not take you to visit your grannie again if you canna behave better.'

This was bad enough—for I knew sooner or later she would slap them and then they would yell their heads off—but presently one of those ubiquitous train bores swayed along the gangway and flopped into the seat next to me. I looked sternly out of the window but it was no good. He felt chatty.

'Cold, innit?' he said. He smelt of whisky.

'Ungh,' I mumbled.

'Looks like snow.'

'Ungh.'

'Cheer up, lassie, dinna look so glum. It'll soon be Christmas.'

'I'm perfectly cheerful,' I snapped unwisely.

'I can see, I can see, I wasnae born yesterday. I've a daughter mysel and I aye ken when there's something on her mind.'

I grunted.

'Want some lemonade. I'm thirsty, Mum,' said one of the children.

'So'm I,' bleated the other.

'You bairns'll be the death of me,' said the mother but eventually she gave way and took them off to the buffet.

The man then offered me a cigarette which I haughtily refused.

'Where do you come frae?' he asked.

'Edinburgh.'

'You don't talk as if you came frae Edinburgh. You talk as if you came frae London.'

'Well, I don't,' I said untruthfully.

'No need to take offence, lassie. Whereabouts in Edinburgh? I'm an Edinburgh man mysel.'

He droned on till I could bear it no longer. I looked at my watch and jumped to my feet as if I had suddenly remembered something and went to find another seat. But the next compartment was full so in the end I stood in the corridor, hating the whole human race.

When, at long last, the train arrived at Waverley, it had begun to snow and I walked slowly up the steep street, half blinded by whirling flakes, as sharp and cold as frozen arrows. I pulled up my hood and plunged my hands into my pockets, thinking bitterly: 'The end of a perfect day.' But I could not resist pausing half-way up the Mound to look down on the lights of Princes Street, each surrounded by a swarm of grey flakes like moths. Beautiful, cold, unfriendly, granite-hearted Edinburgh!

Offices, shops, banks and tenements loomed black and mysterious behind the snow; the flood-lit castle on its craggy base was like a dramatic backcloth to some wild romantic opera. Cities stop being civilised in the snow and I responded by wishing I could be wild and romantic too, stab my faithless lover, pour out my feelings in impassioned verse (or song), before flinging myself off the battlements. But, alas, I was ordinary Emma Langham, famous for her common-sense and I knew that however desperate I felt I would continue to go to school, study for my exams, house-keep for Richard and probably not even lose my appetite.

Already common-sense was creeping up on me. What was I making such a fuss about? Alastair had been glad to see me; he had introduced me to his friends which was really much more complimentary than keeping me a secret. He had kissed me and held my hand in the cinema; he had said 'See you soon'; he had so completely forgiven me for my foolish behaviour that he didn't even think it worth discussing.

You have a nasty character, I told myself, sternly. Not only are you jealous and possessive but you're a worrier, an introspective egotistical bore with an outsize inferiority complex, sodden with self-pity, and if you go on like this you'll probably fail your exams and not get into university at all.

When I reached home I was more or less in my right mind and I walked upstairs stiff with determination to behave as usual, cook supper, sing if requested, and to spend the rest of the time studying.

Richard and I kept a sort of inter-com. slate in the kitchen where we left messages for each other.

I had written this morning:

'Off to Glasgow. Don't know when I'll be back.'

Now I read underneath:

'See if I care. Out to supper myself.' Obviously Pauline was keeping him up to roystering at the weekend and I was pleased to find that she had won her own way with dignity and independence.

As I put on the kettle Joe came in:

'Emma, I think Peter has got flu,' he said.

'Have you sent for the doctor?'

'Not yet.'

'Do you want me to come up and see him?'

'Oh please, Emma. You would be a ministering angel.'

I found Peter in bed. You cannot tell when a black face is pale but I put my hand on his forehead and it was much hotter than normal. I smoothed his bed, turned his pillow, gave him aspirin and hot lemon, and told him firmly that I was going to call the doctor.

'No,' said Peter feebly, 'I am all right.'

'What nonsense. Who is your doctor?'

'The student health service will send one,' said Joe, hovering nervously round the bed. Honestly, for medical students they were both pretty clueless, I thought.

'I don't want a doctor,' repeated Peter.

'I don't care what you want. But I'm not having you lying here moaning, unattended.'

'O.K., O.K.'

So I went downstairs and phoned the Student Health Centre and then I cooked omelettes for Joe and myself.

'What would we do without you, Emma,' said Joe admiringly. I purred.

What with eating our supper, dealing with the doctor, nipping out to an all-night chemist to get a prescription made up (Joe, not me) the evening passed so quickly I had no time to think about myself.

It was only when we were having a mug of coffee in my room, and Joe started asking me personal questions that I remembered, and even then it was oddly comforting, because Joe could not imagine any problems not directly concerned with being black or being hungry.

'You have been to Glasgow to see your friend?' he

asked me. 'The one who does not take you to conferences?'

'Oh he would if I wanted to go,' I said quickly.

'Why do you not want to go?'

'I have enough problems of my own,' I said flippantly. 'I don't feel qualified to cope with other peoples.'

'What sort of problems?'

'Oh Civil Liberties, the plight of political prisoners in Greece and South Africa, that sort of thing.'

'I meant your own.'

'I suppose they're not important really,' I said reluctantly. And indeed at the moment they seemed rather on the level of magazine problem pages:

'I met a nice boy on holiday and he said he loved me and now he is beginning to cool off. How can I make him love me again?'

'What are you doing for Christmas?' I asked, to change the subject.

'There are many kind people who offer hospitality to foreign students—but I do not like charity.'

'Hospitality isn't charity,' I said indignantly.

'You think I am too sensitive?'

'Yes, I do. People want to be kind to each other, it's just that it's sometimes difficult to know exactly how.'

'Would you be kind to a foreign student?'

'Only if I liked him,' I said honestly, 'otherwise it might seem as though I was only doing my Christian duty and that would be insulting.'

'How well you understand. But in any case this Christmas Peter and I are lucky. We have an Indian friend who is married and has a big room. They will cook a huge curry and we will drink much beer.'

I sympathised with Joe but all the same I thought that kindness, real kindness, ought to be encouraged and not sneered at. Perhaps this was one of the awful things about a divided society—that no one could take kindness at its face value.

I wasn't being kind to Joe because he was black. I was just being friendly because I liked him. And yet, when he had asked me about my problems, I'd cut him short as if I did not consider him capable of appreciating my delicate sensibilities.

So I told him a little about my difficulties with Alastair, but described them as ironically as I could.

'I keep feeling,' I finished up, 'as if I were his pet lamb.'

To my astonishment and chagrin, Joe burst into hearty laughter.

'You, a pet lamb,' he spluttered, 'but Peter and I were so nervous about you coming here. Richard said you would rule us with a rod of iron.'

I laughed too, but all the same I felt indignant at the thought of my character being vilified before I had even appeared.

'That is why we are so tidy in the kitchen,' Joe said with a sly twinkle. 'But about your friend. My guess is that he is older and more clever than you. But in a few years' time you will be just as clever as he is. And then your problems will exist no longer. Some things, dear Emma, *are* just a matter of age.'

'I suppose so.'

'Now if I were to fall in love with a Scottish girl, a few years would make no difference.'

In a way I thought that if Alastair and I were black and white (or vice versa) it would be much simpler because then I would be aware of the precise dangers.

'It may not be age, it may be character,' I said gloomily. 'Characters change.'

'Do they? I thought they only developed.'

'My poor Emma, cheer up and tell me what you do for Christmas? Are you going home?'

'Oh yes,' I replied happily, 'I'm going to the island.' And I told him about my scatty family and the art gallery and the beautiful sunsets and the preposterous weather. 'And Alastair's coming too,' I added.

But when Joe had gone I remembered: In Glasgow today neither Alastair nor I had mentioned Christmas. Perhaps he was changing his mind about that too.

16

When I awoke the next morning I was gradually aware that it was much lighter than usual. Of course, it was Sunday, and I could get up at a respectable hour. And then I remembered. The snow. I sprang out of bed and even before I lit the fire or put on my dressing gown I pulled the curtains and looked out on to a white strange world. Thick white window ledges glittered in the electric light. A sycamore tree looked as though it were loaded with blossom. The sun had not yet risen but there was a faint glow in the sky which made the dark hump of Arthur's seat even darker by contrast.

I scrambled into my clothes and took a cup of coffee into Richard.

'Richard, look, the snow!'

'Erggh.'

'Look. It's marvellous.'

Richard opened one eye and shut it again.

'Go away. I'm asleep.'

'No, you're not. Here's your coffee. Do sit up and look.'

'Middle of the night,' muttered Richard thickly.

'It's not. It's morning. The sun's just rising.'

I lit his fire while he grumbled and mumbled but eventually sat up.

'How can you be merry and bright so early,' he complained, sipping his coffee. 'My God, I've just remembered, it's Sunday. You deserve to be strangled.'

'Look,' I said, pressing my face against the window pane.

'You're right. It is rather splendid,' he agreed at last.

'I wish we could go tobogganing—or ski-ing.'

'Do you know anyone with a toboggan?'

'I'll ask John.'

I brought in toast and boiled eggs, our favourite Sunday breakfast, somehow I never had the time or the inclination during the week.

'Poor Peter's got flu,' I told Richard. 'I had to get the doctor.'

'Good for you. Did you enjoy your visit to Glasgow?'

'Hmm.'

'More football?'

'No, the pictures.'

'Pauline and I went to a party.'

'Nice?'

'Pleasant but unremarkable.'

'The polite standing-up sort with wine in wine glasses or the rough sitting-on-the-floor sort with beer in jam jars?'

'Wine in plastic mugs.'

'If you've got some sixpences I'll do the phoning while you get dressed.'

'Emma the organiser!'

'Lucky for you and everyone else that I am.'

It was only Alastair who reduced me to a jelly of incompetence and inferiority, I thought sadly, as I ran downstairs to ring John. He sounded sleepy but the moment he realised it was me speaking his voice changed to a delighted 'Emma, how marvellous.' Yes, he knew a friend with a toboggan, yes, he would meet us at the Braid Hills at eleven o'clock. Then I rang Pauline who sounded even sleepier but I bullied her into coming. Then I hurried upstairs to find out how Peter was, make his bed and to instruct Joe to keep him well supplied with drinks.

There was just time to prepare a huge panful of vegetable soup and to tell Joe to turn the gas off in a couple of hours time though I did not think it would be ruined if he forgot.

At last Richard and I set out together on foot because it seemed such a waste to take the car when we could slither through the thick powdery snow, our breath coming out like little puffs of smoke and feeling that exhilarating sensation of exercise in clear frosty air. The streets, being Sunday, were mostly deserted but here and there were groups of small boys, in woollen caps and wellington boots, snowballing. Some of them threw snowballs at us and we chased them and pelted them back.

'Cheeky little ruffians,' snorted Richard.

It was a splendid day. The sun shone, the snow glittered; dogs and children romped; some people had skis and others, like us, toboggans. John and I took it in turns with Richard and Pauline, and in between we laughed and joked and snowballed each other. It was impossible to feel anything except perfect happiness. It was impossible not to invite John back with us to share the soup with mounds and mounds of chips, which we ate messily in our fingers.

And when it came time for him to go home it seemed churlish not to allow him to kiss me when he wanted to so much. So I kissed him, warmly and gratefully, for having been a part of my happy day, and it was oddly moving to feel him tremble and to hear him whisper: 'Oh Emma, I love you so much.'

'See you tomorrow,' I said prosaically.

'Oh yes!' And he bounded down the steps into the snow, waving gaily.

And at that moment my happiness abruptly vanished. I shivered and closed the front door. Alastair's absence was like a physical pain. That foolish meaningless kiss— meaningless to me, that is—had re-awakened my yearning for Alastair's kisses, for his arms round me, for his voice telling me he loved me And at the same time I realised that if he had been with us on the Braid Hills I would not have enjoyed myself so unselfconsciously. I would have been worrying about his reactions, studying his words, and dreading his departure.

With these perplexing thoughts I walked slowly back upstairs and began preparing to go to bed.

17

When I went to school on Monday I discovered to my dismay that I was now regarded as John's girl.

'So glad to hear about you and John,' whispered Elizabeth to me slyly.

'What do you mean?'

'He phoned Nigel and Nigel phoned me.'

'What about, for goodness' sake. We just went tobogganing together, with my brother and his girlfriend.'

'That's not what I heard.' Elizabeth managed to look smug and conspiratorial at the same time.

'There's nothing else to hear,' I said crossly.

'Oh all right, have it your own way, but after all you can tell me, I'm your friend, I won't broadcast it if you don't want me to.'

'Not half you won't,' I said silently to myself, but aloud: 'John's imagining things. I made everything perfectly clear.'

'O.K., O.K.,' said Elizabeth huffily.

John himself was lurking in the corridor in order to have a private word with me before I went into class.

'I wish we could go tobogganing again today,' he murmured sentimentally.

'The snow's melting.'

'That doesn't stop me wishing. Though I got a row when I arrived home. Mum had my supper waiting.'

'Hard luck,' I said, despising him.

'But I'll come round this evening.'

'You can't. I've got to work,' I said, totally outraged at being taken for granted.

'I'll help you.'

Before I could brush him off the bell rang for registration and after that I had my first English paper, a sort of rehearsal for our Highers in May.

I was so ruffled that it took me several minutes to concentrate on the paper. 'Read and consider the questions carefully before beginning to write,' said the instructions and then, idiotically and unnecessarily, 'Write as clearly and interestingly as you can.' As if anyone would write illegibly and boringly on purpose.

The questions (it was composition) had obviously been designed with me in mind.

'Describe the impact on you of

(i) the experience of being let down by someone in whom you have had trust

OR

(ii) the realisation that it has become necessary to change your present way of life.'

OR

but I could not read any further. Alastair, in whom I had trusted absolutely, had let me down. Without him or the hope of seeing him I would have to change my way of life.

I gazed despairingly round the room. Should I really

write about Alastair, our brief moments of togetherness during the summer, our many moments of friction, our desperate goodbyes on railway stations?

I went on reading.

'Imagine you are a BBC commentator touring an area you know well for a particular purpose....' That was better. I would write about Stranday, my lovely crazy peaceful island. I would imagine myself as someone who had grown up there and was now paying a visit after several years. I was on the boat on a grey misty spring day, arriving at the jetty; the wind would suddenly blow the mist away, the sun would reveal the hills, the sea, the wild daffodils and the golden hawthorn buds exploding into green. And there would be my old (imaginary) father planting his potatoes, and my old (imaginary) mother taking bannocks off the girdle. How Aunt Patsy and Stephen would giggle.

I wrote 'Return to Stranday' at the top of the page and began writing. Not for anything would I tell them (the examiners, teachers, all the sort of people who judged exam papers and who would never understand in a million years how anyone really felt when they were let down by someone they trusted) the truth. I would just write 'as clearly and as interestingly as I could.'

So I did and I thought, with all the modesty I could summon up, that I had probably got an 'A'.

The next paper was just interpretation and grammar and did not involve my feelings. After all, I thought to myself, the examiners were only judging my handwriting, my ability to be interesting and that vague unidentifiable something called intelligence; they weren't judging me as a human being or my sincerity or the validity of my ideas. And, almost for the first time, I understood Aunt Patsy's contempt for formal education and exam results. In the last analysis she was probably right but I was too much affected by vanity and by my desire to prove myself worthy (in their sense of the word) of a university place, not to play along and to do the things expected of me. All the same I felt a little disgusted with myself and slightly guilty for having falsified life on the island.

I did not know anyone, except Alastair, who would share my ambivalent feelings. Richard and Pauline were lucky enough to be studying a subject where their real attitudes did count, but the majority of my fellow students had a simple straightforward desire to pass exams, so that they would get satisfactory jobs when they left school.

And I had absolutely no idea what I wanted to do after I left school. Perhaps my interest in archaeology was just a pet lamb-ish desire to do what Alastair did. All the same, I had some longing, which I couldn't identify, to work at something interesting and useful which wasn't teaching or nursing or typing. I hoped I would find out when—and if—I got to university.

Now I had to find John and stop him spreading the absurd rumours that we were a couple.

I had finished my paper slightly before time and had been walking rather drearily round the concrete playground waiting for the dinner bell to ring. When it did at last ring he was one of the first to come dashing out, looking eagerly for me.

'Emma!' he called delightedly. 'Gosh, it's cold. Let's

go and buy some soup.'

'What on earth have you been telling Nigel?' I came straight to the point.

'Why? I—I only—' he stammered, blushing furiously.

'The whole school's talking about me,' I exaggerated. 'And I made it perfectly clear to you at the beginning that I was in love with someone else.'

'But I thought—I thought—after yesterday—'

'Nothing has changed,' I said fiercely.

'But—you kissed me,' muttered John, looking so stricken, that I couldn't help feeling sorry for him.

'Oh John!' I said helplessly.

'Don't you like me a little bit more than you did?'

If only he wouldn't be so humble and so beseeching. (Did I appear like that to Alastair?)

'Of course I like you,' I said crossly, 'I like you very much. I thought we were friends. But if you go round telling people—'

'It was only Nigel. And I told him in strictest confidence.'

'Well, he told Elizabeth in strictest confidence and she told the entire class, all in strictest confidence too, no doubt.'

'Please don't be angry with me, Emma.'

I gave up and weakly allowed him to buy me soup and a buttered roll while I joined in the general groaning which always takes place during exams. It is a pure matter of form and the people who have done best always groan the loudest. In the afternoon we had the literature paper in which I wrote about Shakespeare's use of clowns (with special reference to Touchstone in *As You Like It*) about romantic poetry as exemplified by Keats and discussed a gloomy novel by Graham Greene. Adequate but not brilliant, I told myself, going into the cloakroom for my duffel.

'I'll give you a lift home,' said John, appearing from nowhere.

I shook my head.

'Can I come round later this evening?'

'I told you I have to work.'

'I could ask you questions.'

'I can only revise by myself. It's what I'm used to.'

John sighed and I nearly relented but no, it would be much more cruel to encourage him. I smiled, but in a faintly abstracted way, and walked to the bus stop.

Mrs. Thomson nobbled me when I opened the front door.

'They've taken Peter to hospital,' she said importantly. 'The doctor was here this morning—said he was gey bad and needed proper medical care.'

'Oh, poor Peter.'

'Well Joe's got his work and you're at school and I don't have the time to look after him.'

'No, of course not.'

'He'll be better off in hospital. I didna like the responsibility and that's a fact. I hope none of the rest of you gets the flu. See you eat proper meals, Emma, and wrap up warm when you go out.'

'Oh I will, Mrs. Thomson. Is Peter in the Infirmary? I'll go round with some fruit some time.'

'Ward 15. I've written it down on the telephone pad. My man was in Ward 24 with his coronary,' she went on and I knew that she was going to retail the grisly details of his death, so I quickly interrupted:

'I must dash upstairs and do some work. We're in the middle of exams.'

'Have a cuppa tea first. I've just put the kettle on.'

'Thanks awfully, Mrs. Thomson, but I honestly haven't time.'

As I turned to go the telephone rang. I looked at it with a beating heart. Could it be for me? No, of course it couldn't. I was home early on account of the exam and no one (naturally I meant Alastair) would expect to find me there. But as I was nearer to the instrument than Mrs. Thomson I lifted the receiver and said 'Hello.'

Peep peep peep went the pips and then 'Is Emma there?' came Alastair's voice.

'Alastair!' I cried, my knees almost buckling under me with excitement.

'What's the matter? Your voice sounds funny.'

'I'm so surprised.'

'I'm surprised, too, to find you at home. I thought I'd just have to leave a message. You see I'm in Edinburgh.'

'In Edinburgh?' I repeated incredulously.

'Yes. Some of us came through to see the exhibition of Roman remains in the Natural History Museum. Have you been yet?'

'I've been busy with exams.'

'Do you want to join us now?'

Did I? I paused before saying yes. I did not really want to see Alastair in a public place among all his friends. I wanted to see him alone.

'I've just this second got back from school,' I explained.

'Why don't you come round here when you're through and I'll make us something to eat.'

'Don't bother about food. I won't be able to stay long. I'll be with you at the back of five. Bye for now.'

'Bye.'

Mrs. Thomson had discreetly withdrawn—though I bet she listened to every word. I danced upstairs singing one of Richard's favourite Purcell songs 'to celebrate, to celebrate this high holiday' at the top of my voice. I had an hour to wash, change, tidy and pop something casual and inconspicuous in the oven. History revision would have to wait.

18

It was five o'clock. My room was warm, tidy and inviting.
Soup was simmering on the stove and bread, butter and
cheese laid on the tray so that we could eat with a mini-
mum of fuss. I had changed my clothes about five times,
at one moment deciding that I would be as smart as possible in my jersey frock and at another to be colourful
and casual in trousers and a sweater. At the last moment
I put on my monk's habit to show my independence,
reflecting as I did so, that no one noticed clothes less than
Alastair and it was probably all wasted effort.

I tramped restlessly round the room, twitched curtains
and cushions, switched on the radio and then switched it
off again in case I might miss hearing the door bell. I
opened my door and hovered on the landing.

It was a quarter past five and I began to imagine all
the reasons why Alastair might be delayed. The exhibition might be so interesting that he had simply forgotten
the time; his friends might have cajoled him into popping
into a pub for a quick pint; then I wondered if he had
rung up at half past three not expecting me to be in,
what message he had intended to leave—for me to meet
him in some café or to join him at the Natural History

Museum most probably. Perhaps he had not wanted to come round in order to see me alone but I had forced his hand. Had he hesitated before replying? Why hadn't he let me know sooner?

I groaned. I was relapsing into that nervous suspicious state of mind which would make unselfconscious behaviour impossible. If only he had not kept me waiting! Grimly I sat down at my table and took out my history books so that I would appear to be happily working instead of unhappily waiting. I started studying an old exam paper: 'Why did Spanish greatness decline so markedly after the death of Philip II in 1598?' 'Did the Revolutions of 1848 produce any worthwhile results?' 'Account for the aggressive nature of Mussolini's foreign policy.' But it was impossible to concentrate. Philip II, the 1848 Revolutions and Mussolini swam around in my head in a confused jumble.

Alastair did not arrive until a quarter to six. I heard the front door bell and willed myself to sit still and not rush out to answer it. Then came Alastair's footsteps on the stairs and his knock on my door. I turned to say 'Hullo' with a perfect blend of casualness and warmth.

'I say,' said Alastair, holding me at arm's length, 'have I wandered into a monastery?'

'Do you like it?'

'It's a little strange at first.'

He kissed my cheek and his lips were cold from the outside air and so were his hands.

He took off his jacket and stood with his back to the fire.

'What was the exhibition like?'

'Good. You ought to have come.'

'I was too exhausted from writing essays.'

'How did the exam go?'

'Nothing special, just routine stuff. It's history I'm worried about—you have to know so much but not enough for it to be really interesting.'

'I know.'

Was our conversation always so stilted and boring? If only he'd kiss me properly and tell me how much he had missed me, but he seemed restless and ill at ease and just stood there, asking questions about Richard and Pauline and even the weather.

'We went tobogganing on Sunday,' I said desperately, 'on the Braid Hills. It was fabulous.'

'Why not ski-ing?'

'Too expensive to hire the equipment.'

Alastair looked as though he were going to say something and then changed his mind.

'I'll get us something to eat,' I said.

'Emma, I told you not to bother.'

'It wasn't any bother. I have to eat too.'

'I'm just not hungry.'

'But—' I began, thinking of my soup bubbling on the stove, then I controlled myself.

'I'll take a cup of coffee if you're making any,' said Alastair ungraciously.

I went over to him, putting my hands on his shoulders, and searching his face for signs of his feelings. Why couldn't I be like Pauline, tweak his hair, call him a barbarian and laugh him out of his bad humour?

'Kiss me,' I said, 'and then I'll make you some coffee.'

Alastair laughed, unnaturally I thought, and took me in his arms.

I wanted to say 'I love you' but it was the sort of thing one could only say when one was absolutely sure of the response.

'Coffee,' I said brightly, going into the kitchen, hoping that Alastair would follow me and then hoping he wouldn't in case he noticed the supper preparations.

'You saved me from Mrs. Thomson, ringing up when you did,' I told him. 'She was just inveigling me into her kitchen for a cuppa.'

'What's wrong with her?'

'Nothing but she will talk about her operations. Poor Peter has had to go into the infirmary with flu and this set off grisly reminiscences.'

I tried to chatter amusingly but I was still on edge and silences kept falling, not nice warm companionable silences, but chilly nervous silences during which my mouth dried up and my heart beat painfully.

'I can't wait for Christmas,' I said at last. 'We're planning to travel up on the 23rd, is that O.K. for you?'

At this Alastair gave a nervous start.

'That was one of the things I wanted to talk to you about,' he said.

Foreboding filled me. I made a questioning noise.

'Would you be awfully upset if I didn't come?'

'Why? What's happened?' my voice croaked.

'There's a chance of going ski-ing,' Alastair said rapidly, not meeting my eyes. 'One of the chaps has borrowed a Dormobile that holds eight and we were going to drive up to Glenshee and stay in the hostel there. It's a fantastic opportunity. I've always wanted to go ski-ing and this is the first time I've been able to afford it.'

I simply could not speak. I walked over to the window and gazed out into the darkness, blinking back tears, absolutely determined not to break down.

'You do understand, don't you?' went on Alastair. 'I mean the island will still be there in the summer but the snow won't. I know how much you want to be with your family but you'll have just as good a time without me.'

The sheer dishonesty made me shake with rage. I wanted to yell and scream and call him all the names I could think of but all I said was: 'I see.'

'I wish you could come too but it's just chaps. And in any case you wouldn't want to miss going to the island, would you?'

'No.'

'There'll be lots of other opportunities for being together.'

'Will there?'

'Oh Emma, don't be like that. You make me feel such a heel.'

'Well you are,' I said silently.

'I'll only be away for a fortnight and then we'll meet to celebrate the New Year together.'

Keeping my voice as steady as possible, and biting my lower lip to keep it from trembling, I said at last:

'You really mean you want to chuck me, don't you?'

'No, Emma, of course not. It's just as I said, I've always wanted to go ski-ing and it would be crazy to turn down this opportunity. Now cheer up, there's a good girl.

You'll have a marvellous time and then we'll meet to swap experiences. I'll send you a postcard. Now I must fly. I'm meeting the others at the station at seven o'clock. Thanks for the coffee.'

I handed him his jacket, allowed myself to be kissed, and waved him goodbye from the top of the stairs.

19

It is difficult to describe the rest of the week. There was someone, answering to my name, who got up in the morning and went to school, who sat the history exam—and the French and the Geography exams—who bought bread and eggs and fish; who cooked supper and washed up afterwards. But she bore no relation to the real Emma underneath who re-lived, again and again, that humiliating scene with Alastair. Again and again I heard those cruel words 'Would you be awfully upset if I didn't come?' 'You do understand, don't you?' 'Now cheer up, there's a good girl.' And worst of all 'I'll send you a postcard.' Each time I remembered that little casual sentence —to be fobbed off with a postcard after the promise of ten glorious days together—the pain was so intense I almost yelled aloud. But I did not cry; not a single tear. Nor did I say one word about my feelings to anyone.

Richard and I had always respected each other's silent moods. A brother and sister living together did not have to make polite conversation when they did not feel like it. When Richard was composing he hardly spoke for days on end and I daresay he presumed that I was totally involved in my exams.

He did once say:

'You're not sickening for flu, are you?'

'Certainly not.'

'Don't overdo this work thing.'

'I'm not.'

Once I came very near to bursting out the truth. Pauline had come to supper and naturally we talked of our Christmas plans.

'Have you fixed the arrangements with your footballing friend?' Richard asked.

For a moment I was tempted to tell them that I had been jilted, stood up, let down, chucked—one of those bitter humiliating expressions—but I found I could not bear to put it into words.

'Alastair?' I said flatly. 'Oh, didn't I tell you? He can't come after all. He's going ski-ing.'

'Oh, the rotten beast,' exploded Pauline. 'Are you dreadfully disappointed?'

'It was too good an opportunity to miss,' I explained. My voice sounded a long way off but quite steady.

'I'd like to have a go at ski-ing myself,' said Richard quickly. 'We might all go some weekend if we can spare the time and the car behaves.'

'That would be fantabulous,' agreed Pauline.

They both looked at me rather nervously.

'Yes,' I said limply. Then I got up and went into my room where I spent most evenings lying on my bed staring at the ceiling.

Presently there was a knock at the door and Pauline came in.

'Emma!'

'Hmm?'

'I'm sorry I was tactless. I didn't know about Alastair.'

'What about him?'

'That you'd broken up.'

'I don't think we have. He just isn't coming for Christmas, that's all.'

Pauline sighed.

'I know how you feel,' she said, 'honestly, I do. I wish you'd talk to me.'

I thought longingly of telling Pauline everything, of crying, of being comforted but there was something rock-like inside me, my pride perhaps, that would not move. How could she understand? How could happy people ever understand unhappy people?

'There's nothing to say,' I said.

'Richard's worried about you.'

'There's no need. I'm perfectly all right.'

'We'll have a marvellous Christmas in any case. I do hope Patsy and Stephen will like me. I know I'll like them.'

'They will,' I said.

How was I going to bear Christmas when every second I would miss Alastair and when I would have to make superhuman efforts to appear normally cheerful? Of course I still wanted to see Aunt Patsy and Stephen and Vanessa but they seemed so far away, so unreal that they were less important than characters in a favourite book. I did not believe in their reality.

Eventually Pauline left me and I went on staring at the ceiling hearing Alastair's voice saying, 'I'll send you a postcard.'

The worst day was Friday. The last exam was finished and I came home to find the house empty. I dumped the shopping on the kitchen table and stood wearily staring at the stove, wondering if I could be bothered to make myself a cup of coffee. It seemed too much effort. I wandered into Richard's room, fingered the music on the piano, and stared at the pile of manuscripts on the table. How lucky he was to be so totally absorbed in his music!

Then I wandered into my own room and absent-mindedly lit a match for the fire. In the moment between lighting the match and applying it there was a spurt of sickly-smelling gas. That was how some people committed suicide, turning on the gas, closing the window and laying a blanket under the door. You lay down, with your head on a cushion and fell asleep to wake no more. But the smell was too unpleasant. You would need to be drunk first.

Suddenly I was horror-stricken by my thoughts. I lit the fire and went over to the window, gazing at the forlorn garden, the leafless trees, the lights from other lonely bedsitters pricking the dusk.

I wished Richard would come home. I wished I had allowed John to give me a lift. I wished even that Mrs. Thomson had invited me into her kitchen. Anything would be better than solitude.

Perhaps Joe would be in and I could go and ask him how Peter was. I walked slowly upstairs and knocked on their door but there was no reply. I entered the room, which was comfortless and unnaturally tidy, the two beds neatly made; the bookcase full of medical books; shoes in a row under the wardrobe. Peter and Joe might feel occasionally lonely in a hostile white world but eventually they would return to be useful to their own people and that would make them happy regardless of any personal disappointments they might suffer. Tomorrow I would buy some fruit and take it round to Peter.

On the table between the beds was a bottle of pills and I idly picked them up and looked at the label. 'One at night as directed' I read in the chemist's squiggly handwriting. They were probably sleeping pills. That would be another and less disagreeable way of dying.

People committed suicide when the balance of their minds was disturbed. Was the balance of my mind disturbed?

Dispassionately I surveyed my situation. There were two possibilities, equally dismal. One, that I would never see Alastair again and would live a life without love, in which work would be pointless because I was not sure that I wanted to be an archaeologist on my own. Two, that I would continue this painful unsatisfactory relationship, forever torn by fear and worry and dread, always waiting for telephone calls and letters, always sobbing on railway stations or making humiliating scenes.

No, the balance of my mind was not disturbed at all. I was thinking lucidly and matter-of-factly. I was seeing the situation exactly as it was and the most reasonable action to take would be to swallow sleeping pills or turn on the gas.

I had wandered downstairs like a sleep walker and now I found myself in the kitchen, mechanically unpacking the shopping and putting it tidily away, bread in the bin, butter in the fridge, eggs in their cardboard containers. I poured a glass of water and drank it thirstily. It was curious how one's body seemed to have a life of its own. Passing the mirror as I returned to my own room I caught sight of myself as if I were a stranger. Could that pale face really be mine? I felt frightened, like Alice when she is in the wood and cannot remember her name. I could remember my name, Emma Langham, but I just could not remember who that Emma was. And there was no one to tell me.

I went into the passage and called 'Richard! Richard!' but the house was still empty.

Still in a sleep-walkerish way I began slowly to undress, putting away my school clothes as tidily as I always did. But just as I was going to climb into bed I discovered that instead of putting on my pyjamas I had put on my monk's habit.

'Just habit,' I murmured to myself and giggled weakly at the pun. This was another proof that the balance of my mind was not disturbed. But to make absolutely sure I began repeating history dates, the repeal of the Combination Acts, of the three Reform Bills, of the Boer War, of the General Strike, of the battle of Austerlitz. So far so good. But I could not remember the date of the Edict of Nantes—was it 1598 or 1589?

I could not possibly settle down until I had checked in my European history book. So I sat down at my work table and began searching in a desultory way, growing more and more tired.

'I'm tired,' I said aloud, 'poor Emma is tired,' and I folded my arms and laid my head upon them. The exams

were over so why on earth was I bothering about history
dates? I couldn't remember now what I had been looking
up or why, only that it had been terribly important. I
would have a nap and when I woke up my head would
be clear again and I would remember. I crept into sleep
as under a large fluffy eiderdown that blotted out everything.

20

I dreamt I was swimming in the sea off our beach at
Stranday. At first it was beautifully calm and gentle and
I swam effortlessly with long even strokes that sent me
gliding through the clear green water. And then when
I turned to swim to the shore, the sea became stormy and
enormous waves broke over my head. My strokes became
taut and flurried as I struggled, my breath came in gasps,
and again and again a heavy foaming breaker swamped
me, and the shore seemed to get farther and farther away.
Then through the thunder of the waves I heard a voice
calling: 'Emma! Emma!'

I woke up with a convulsive movement. There was
indeed a voice calling 'Emma'—it was Stephen's. And
he was standing beside me, shabby and familiar, his face
crinkled into a welcoming smile.

Before I had time to think or speak I flung myself into
his arms and tears burst out of me like a waterfall. He
held me warmly and tightly and through my sobs I could
hear him saying in affectionate bewilderment: 'Emma,
darling Emma, what on earth's the matter? Oh my poor
love, Emma, tell me what's the matter? There, there, my
darling, don't cry.'

It was so lovely to cry that I never wanted to stop but at last, of course, I did. Stephen handed me his handkerchief and I mopped my face, mumbling tremulously: 'I'm sorry. I'm awfully sorry.'

'Is something terribly wrong?'

'Yes—no—not really—it's only—' Oh damn, I was going to start crying again.

'Just tell me quickly, is anyone dead or dying or in prison, you or Richard I mean?'

'No, no, nothing like that.'

'Thank God,' said Stephen, mopping his own brow, and lighting a cigarette. He gazed at me with loving concern and stroked my hair back behind my ears.

'Listen, Emma. What you need is food and drink. I'm convinced of it. You look delightful in this curious garb but I want you to look female and gay. So change your clothes and wash your face and then I shall take you out to supper. Right?'

'But I look so awful,' I began.

'Nonsense. You're fortunately not one of these females who look all pink and sodden after weeping. You just look like a little damp dewy flower—' he began to laugh, 'a marsh orchid or something.'

'Oh Stephen.'

'Go and change. Then we shall eat something delicious. I haven't eaten something delicious in a restaurant for months. And during—or after—the meal you can tell me all your troubles from A to Z. Hurry.'

Oh the relief of being taken charge of. I drenched my face in cold water and patted it dry. Stephen was right. I didn't, thank goodness, look pink and sodden. I put on my green jersey frock, my copper medallion, brushed my hair, darkened my eyelashes, and dabbed my birthday perfume behind my ears.

Stephen examined me critically, when I re-appeared.

'Now you look too smart to go out with a shabby middle-aged painter,' he grumbled.

He could have been wearing his old paint-stained trousers and his shiny-in-places donkey jacket for all I cared. Actually he was wearing a sagging tweed suit with a charcoal grey polo-necked sweater, but he was Stephen and that was the only thing that mattered.

'Eccentric but distinguished,' I said.

'Bless you. Now put on your coat and off we go.'

'How are Aunt Patsy and Vanessa?' I asked as we went down the stairs, and out into the cold dark street.

'Absolutely fine. I was sent to Glasgow to pick up some Christmas fare and I couldn't resist coming over to see you. I've also been seeing the man who's exhibiting my stuff in the spring.'

This sort of conversation kept us going till we reached an Italian restaurant and we sat down amid chianti bottles, strings of onions, glass decanters with long spouts and lurid views of Palermo and Rome on the walls.

'Do you want to choose or shall I choose for you?'

'You choose. But won't it be terribly expensive?'

'Quiet! Things are looking up. And nothing's too good for my—well, what are you? Niece? Adopted daughter? Down with labels! You're just Emma. My favourite Emma.'

He ordered minestrone with a bowl full of grated parmesan cheese, and then huge escalopes sandwiched between cheese and ham, a green salad, and a jug of red chianti.

I ate gratefully, and sipped my wine and very very gradually I became myself again. I knew my name and I knew who I was.

'Come on. Tell,' said Stephen.

Somehow it wasn't humiliating to tell Stephen, as it would have been to tell Pauline or Richard or anyone else. And as I spoke my thoughts became clear. Alastair had enjoyed my adoration but in a way it made him feel uncomfortable. He had wanted a pleasant, easy relationship, not to start something serious and binding. He liked me, and possibly even loved me a little, but not enough to arrange his life around me.

'I was just his pet lamb,' I told Stephen.

'This is where I would say I'd horsewhip him if I had a horse,' said Stephen, 'or beat him to within an inch of his life if I had a tape measure—do you like the Marx brothers, Emma? But it wouldn't be any good, would it?'

'No.'

'I can only say,' said Stephen, 'that love is a difficult thing. You can't expect to succeed first go. But every time you really do love you learn something.'

'I'll never love anyone again.'

'But you will. You must. You wouldn't think you could write a poem or play a violin sonata or paint a picture without any experience, would you?'

'No, but—'

'But me no buts. Listen, Emma, do you think Patsy was the first woman I ever loved?'

'I suppose not.'

'Of course not. Any more than I was the first man she ever loved.'

'N-no.' It was difficult to grasp. I had always taken it for granted that for them love, marriage and the birth of Vanessa had taken place in orderly sequence.

'Patsy can tell you herself,' said Stephen. 'What she did and thought and felt before we got married, but I'll tell you that I was in love with half a dozen girls, some more, some less, some painful, some joyous, before I realised that Patsy was my one and only.'

'Oh.'

'There was one girl—she was already married—I wanted her to get a divorce but she kept putting it off and putting it off, and we kept meeting and parting, and weeping tears of blood, saying goodbye on railway stations and then ringing up next morning to say it had all been a mistake.'

'She must have been a beast.'

'No, she simply couldn't make up her mind. I learnt a lot, Emma. I saw her not so long ago and I didn't feel at all bitter. I felt grateful. That with her I had known such moments of complete happiness.'

'If only Alastair hadn't said that about the postcard.'

'He's frightened of responsibility, Emma.'

'I suppose so.'

'Now don't tell me you're going to be a man-hater for ever after.'

He poured out the rest of the wine and looked at me, smiling.

'No. I suppose not. If only I didn't feel so ashamed.'

'What have you got to be ashamed of? You have a

loving heart, Emma, and that's nothing to be ashamed of.'

'It doesn't feel like that.'

'Love, love, love,' said Stephen impatiently. 'There are as many kinds as there are people. Sometimes it's reciprocated and then it makes a different kind of love. Sometimes it isn't. But, believe me, Emma, if I may be elderly and portentous, first love is almost always tragic and terrible and agonising. Almost never satisfactory. In fact people who fall in love at the age of sixteen and live happily ever after can be counted on the fingers of one foot. I personally have never met one.'

I looked at him unbelievingly.

'Do you know that poem of Yeats' when he talks about the three women he'd loved? I'm a rotten quoter but I can remember bits. He talks about Lady Gregory with whom he'd had this terrific intellectual companionship, the Irish theatre and all that and says that nothing "could ever come between Mind and delighted mind." And then there was his wife, who obviously took him in hand, and stopped him making a fool of himself so that he could live "labouring in ecstasy." And the third was Maude Gonne, who didn't apparently love him but who inspired some of his most marvellous poems. She was cruel and off-hand and took, as he says, all his youth "with scarce a pitying look" and yet, and that's the line that always stays in my memory, whenever he thinks of her, "up from my heart's root, so great a sweetness flows I shake from head to foot." '

'And that last sort, did you feel that with the girl that was married?'

'I believe I did,' said Stephen musingly, 'I believe I did. Yes, even when I saw her, middle-aged and rather fat and with grey streaks in her hair, a great sweetness did flow.'

'But Aunt Patsy,' I said, horrified.

'Ah, I wouldn't swap one centimetre, one second of my life with Patsy, for any other sort of love. But that doesn't mean I have to falsify my memories. Oh dear, Emma, I am sounding terribly old and philosophical, my memories, dear me, why don't you stop me?'

'But I'm so interested.'

And I thought again of Alastair and wondered which sort of love I had with him. But the pain was a little remote because I was so full of food and a little muzzy from the wine and I had never had such an intimate conversation with Stephen before.

'So you see, Emma, everything we feel is different because we are individuals and yet everything we feel is the same because we are part of the human race. There's comfort somewhere, though I'm not quite sure where. Shall we go?'

So we walked slowly home, me hanging limply on to Stephen's arm, while he told me island gossip and described some of the devilish things Vanessa had been doing now that she was mobile—climbing into the peat basket and smearing toothpaste all over the bathroom floor.

Richard was in and he bounced out of his room saying furiously:

'Emma, where have you been?' before he saw Stephen.

'I took Emma out to dinner.'

'You might at least have left a message,' Richard grumbled.

'I'm sorry.'

'I was hungry too. I had to eat baked beans on toast and I bet you two have been gorging on fillet steak.'

'Escalope actually,' I said, smugly, 'and—'

'No, don't tell me or I'll start being hungry all over again.'

'Have some more baked beans.'

'Do you think,' Stephen asked, 'that I could kip down on your sofa? I was going back to Glasgow tonight but I'd rather stay if you don't mind. I'll just phone the people I was staying with.'

Richard looked at me enquiringly.

'Better?' he asked.

'Much, much better,' I replied.

21

'Today Emma and I are going shopping,' said Stephen at breakfast. 'I am going to buy her a Christmas present. Do you wish to accompany us, Richard?'

Richard shuddered. He detests shopping for anything, except books and music.

'I have more important things to do,' he said.

'Shall we meet for lunch then? Nothing as splendid as last night, I fear, just a dish of something simple and nourishing.'

We arranged to meet at a self-service salad place where you eat as much as you can for 12/6 and then Stephen and I set off down the hill to Princes Street.

'Something pretty to wear for Christmas, I think,' Stephen said, 'a dress, for instance.'

'That would be lovely.'

I had imagined buying something sensible in one of the chain stores, but Stephen whisked me past them to a shop I had never even been into before, as all the things displayed in the windows seemed to cost £20 or more.

'Everything's terribly expensive here,' I warned him.

'Don't fuss.'

'Have we suddenly got rich?'

'Christmas comes but once a year.'

Stephen was a most satisfactory person to shop with. We examined everything, shirts and suits and coats as well as every sort of dress before settling down in the special department for the under twenty-ones.

'Try on absolutely everything you fancy and even some that you don't,' he advised me. 'This for instance.'

'This' was a garment in emerald green suede with a fringed hem.

'I couldn't possibly wear that.'

'Try it for fun.'

He began taking dresses off the rail, white lace, pink and orange stripes, printed corduroy and black velvet; collared an assistant and seated himself in an armchair.

'Mannequin parade,' he ordered. 'Off you go.'

I looked extremely peculiar in the green suede, as if I had strayed out of Sherwood Forest and needed a bow and arrow to complete the outfit. Even the assistant giggled.

The pink and orange stripes clashed dreadfully with my hair and the white lace made me look like a gawky bridesmaid. The corduroy was better, a simple shirt dress in tiny brown and orange flowers.

'Possible, possible,' said Stephen, 'but a bit ordinary.'

Then I tried on the black velvet. I had kept it for the last because I had always had a longing to wear black but had thought that I was not sophisticated enough.

It had a big white lace collar and threequarter-length sleeves with white lace cuffs and there were rows of tiny velvet covered buttons down the front and on the sleeves.

I looked at myself in the mirror and wondered why I

had never worn black before. My face looked paler, my
eyes bigger, my hair redder. At last, at long last, I felt I
had achieved something approaching sex-appeal. If only
Alastair could see me now he would never have decided
to go ski-ing. And I quickly imagined a dramatic scene
with Alastair imploring me to forgive him, telling me
I was the only girl he had ever loved and would ever
love while I smiled mysteriously, saying neither yes nor
no.

I parted the curtains and stood still for a minute, smiling mysteriously at Stephen (for practice) and then
walked slowly towards him, turned round, lifted one
elegant black velvet arm to smooth my hair, and said:
'Well?'

'That's it. Absolutely it,' said Stephen. 'Turn round
again, sit down, no, not like that, gracefully. Now turn
towards me and say something charming.'

'Something charming.'

'You need more eye make-up and a different hair style.
And white lace stockings and black patent shoes with
silver buckles and then you'll have every male within a
radius of ten miles suffering from high blood pressure.'

'Thank you,' I said graciously.

'We'll take the black velvet,' he said to the assistant.

But when I took it off I saw the price tag and nearly
fainted—twenty-two guineas. Stephen couldn't possibly
afford it. The printed corduroy was only £12 and it
would be perfectly adequate. When would I have the
opportunity to wear black velvet?

I hurried into my own clothes and went back to
Stephen.

'Stephen. We can't. Buy the black velvet, I mean. It's much too expensive. Let me have the corduroy instead.'

'Quiet,' said Stephen.

'But it's twenty-two guineas!' I bleated.

'Then you'll have to wear it every day for the next five years.'

'But honestly.'

'For the sake of that black velvet dress I am prepared to starve. Don't be silly, Emma. What's money for if not to buy what you want? I'm going to be rich and famous but if you're rich and famous first you can buy me something beautiful.'

So I allowed the dress to be packed and, though I winced as Stephen signed the cheque, I could not help feeling happy and excited. When Alastair came back from ski-ing I was going to behave entirely differently. I was going to be aloof and mysterious and banish my pet lamb character for ever.

'Now we'll buy the shoes and stockings while we're in the mood,' said Stephen.

So we did and afterwards I bought a cuddly stockinette doll for Vanessa, a pink marble egg for Aunt Patsy, a record token for Richard, and a kaleidoscope for Pauline.

I could not believe I was the same person whom Stephen had rescued on Friday night.

At the same time I knew at the back of my mind that not even the best and kindest of Stephens could solve my problems, and that food and drink and new clothes could only be temporary distractions. Sooner or later I should have to do some serious thinking. But not yet, I told myself, not yet.

Lunch was a pleasant noisy meal but I kept fading out of the conversation to recapture that sensation I had had on first seeing myself in the black dress, when I had been absolutely certain of my female power. If only I'd been wearing it on Monday instead of my monk's habit. And I feverishly tried to plan occasions when I could wear it —at a dance, for instance, or a party, where I would flirt tremendously with every man in sight, except Alastair. He had said we would celebrate New Year together when he came back, and that might mean a party or a meal in a restaurant. I could just see, like a corny advertisement, him gazing across the table at me, his voice husky with passion, saying 'You're beautiful, Emma, you're the most beautiful girl in the world.'

Here, the unlikeliness of the scene made even my imagination balk; I wasn't quite up to giggling but I smiled faintly and Richard said:

'You're very quiet, Emma. Having beautiful thoughts?'

'I'm thinking about my dress.'

'Tell,' urged Pauline.

'No, I'm not going to say a word. It's a Christmas present and I shall wear it for Christmas and surprise you all.'

Now I imagined a far more possible scene. At the last moment Alastair would decide not to go ski-ing and arrive—unheralded—at the cottage. He would be chatting to the others in the kitchen until I floated gracefully down the stairs and glided into the room. There would be sudden hush, a gasp of astonishment.

Stephen was saying that he had to get back to Glasgow.

'I brought some of my pictures with me,' he said, 'and there are a couple of characters who just might buy one. It always looks good to start off an exhibition with a few little red circles.'

So he went to the station and Pauline, Richard and I walked slowly home.

It wasn't until I was in my room that I remembered I had done no weekend shopping and I felt a great disinclination to do so.

Richard was at the piano and Pauline was joining up her oboe.

'I haven't done any food shopping,' I said.

'Plenty of time,' said Richard, doing a couple of arpeggios.

'I don't feel like it, I'm tired,' I said sulkily.

'Have a rest and do it later.'

'I don't see why it always has to be me.'

'I don't mind—' began Pauline but Richard cut her off.

'Well, I do. We've got to practise for the end of term concert.'

'You and your rotten music,' I burst out, 'it's all you ever think of.'

Richard and I seldom quarrelled but when we did it was pretty fierce and, although I knew that I was really venting my bad temper on him quite unjustly, I couldn't stop.

'You're a spoilt brat,' snarled Richard, 'Stephen's been spoiling you with fancy meals and fancy clothes. It's time you took a grip on yourself.'

'Stop it, both of you,' said Pauline, utterly bewildered, for she had never seen us having a slanging match before.

'You're bone selfish,' I shouted.

'Shut up and get out.'

'I will. And I'll stay out.'

'Good.'

I slammed the door till the windows rattled and stamped around my own room, kicking things, and muttering under my breath.

In the end, of course, I did go out but I only bought the bare necessities and nothing special for Sunday lunch.

While I was in the kitchen putting things away Pauline re-appeared and she too had a full shopping bag.

She looked at me nervously and I looked at her. Suddenly I wasn't in a bad temper any more. We both burst into roars of laughter. And she, fortunately, had not bothered about mundane things like bread and butter, she had bought a chicken for Sunday lunch.

22

The first few days at Stranday were so hectic and so hilarious that I did not often have time to remember how unhappy I still was.

The drive to Oban had not been too bad but when we arrived it was pouring with rain and there was a gale-force wind. We had to wait, rather miserably, while the authorities decided whether or not it was safe to cross and this doubt was still in at least Pauline's and my mind while the boat lurched through heaving seas. Pauline was sick, Richard looked green and I lay down with my eyes closed, counting endless five hundreds to propitiate fate.

But when we actually arrived at the cottage everything changed. Stephen was there with mulled wine to welcome us; Aunt Patsy was flapping gently about murmuring: 'Oh dear, I seem to have forgotten bread,' and 'What are we going to stuff the turkey with, Emma?' and Vanessa, darling Vanessa, in a cherry coloured jersey to match her cheeks and blue dungarees to match her eyes, was crawling about, attacking people's shoe laces, strewing carrots all over the kitchen floor, and chewing anything unsuitable she could find.

Aunt Patsy did find the opportunity to say to me, 'I'm so sorry, Emma, that Alastair couldn't come.'

'I'm not sure yet if it was couldn't or didn't want to,' I replied a little grimly.

'Oh dear, aren't men beasts?'

'Don't worry. I shall survive,' I said.

'Of course, but I don't like you to be unhappy.'

'I'm not,' I lied.

So we decorated the Christmas tree, mostly with home-made things, bits of left-over jewelry, and silver painted fir cones; I peeled hundreds of potatoes and biked into Ardloch for the many many things Aunt Patsy had forgotten; Richard and Pauline walked to the farm for extra eggs and milk and were told by the old witch that they were lucky 'it wasn't raining fire and brimstone', her favourite remark; the headmaster of the school, Mr. Kilpatrick, came with a honeycomb and some of his wife's home-made elderberry wine; Stephen brought in enough peat and logs to last for a siege; best of all we filled Vanessa's stocking with fruit and toys. 'No sweets,' said Aunt Patsy fiercely, 'I'm not having her ruin her teeth.'

'But she's only got two,' said Richard.

'It's the principle of the thing.'

The only near catastrophe was on Christmas day when we finally decided to start cooking the turkey and after about half an hour the container of rural gas ran out.

'I told you to see to it,' Aunt Patsy accused Stephen.

'Nonsense. I asked you and you said we were O.K.'

'I didn't. I specially asked you.'

So Stephen and Richard departed on bicycles for Donald-the-Minibus's house for he was the agent on the island. But Donald was already celebrating in the hotel so after a dram or two with Mrs. Donald they followed him to the hotel and there, of course, they had to have several more drams before they could persuade him to return home and deliver us a new container.

Pauline, Aunt Patsy and I, spent the time usefully in putting Vanessa to bed and in arraying ourselves in our best clothes. They admired me in my black dress and I tried my best not to hope that Alastair would suddenly arrive. Dressing up is all very well but one does want someone special to appreciate one's efforts. Pauline wore a long sea-green frock with lots of beads and her hair in a gold snood.

When the men returned Donald could not keep his eyes off her.

'Would you be one of they hippies?' he asked her, his eyes wide with astonishment and curiosity.

'Certainly not,' said Pauline, 'I'm a hard-working music student.'

'Ah, a student,' said Donald, as if that explained everything.

So what with one thing and another we did not sit down to our Christmas feast until about ten o'clock and after it we were too full and too sleepy to do more than stack the dishes and stumble into bed.

But apart from eating and drinking, playing records and cards, talking and laughing, playing with Vanessa and bullying people into doing household chores, I found time to re-discover my island.

I walked along the shore, breathing in the icy air, watching the wicked-looking waves pounding on to the rocks at high tide, throwing up great spumes of spray, and I listened to the gurgle of water being drawn out of the pools and the harsh cries of the gulls. I sat on my special rock where I had met Alastair for the first time and wondered if Susan had gone ski-ing. He had said that their group was 'only chaps' but that did not necessarily mean that Susan had not gone up separately.

I shuddered.

The next day the weather changed abruptly; the wind dropped, the sun shone, and the mist lifted so that I could see the snow-capped mountains on the mainland—even our own two smallish hills were white and glittering against the blue sky. The sea was now navy-blue instead of grey, with little lace-edged waves.

I decided to walk along the road where I had so often walked with Alastair and go up the track to where our dig had been last summer.

Richard and Pauline had gone with Stephen into the gallery where Stephen was knocking up picture frames, Pauline was experimenting with ceramic jewelry and Richard was playing the piano. Aunt Patsy was sitting sleepily in front of the fire trying to read while Vanessa crawled round the room wanting things she couldn't have.

'Going out?' asked Aunt Patsy, as I came in winding a scarf round my neck and looking for my gloves.

'Oh you beast,' I told Vanessa who was sucking one. 'It's sopping wet. Yes, I thought I'd go for a walk.'

'Vanessa's bored,' said Aunt Patsy meaningfully.

'Oh.'

'She'd like to go for a walk too, wouldn't you, monster?'

Vanessa, who had just been going to yell at being deprived of her glove, looked up. She could not speak yet, apart from vague noises that might have been Mam-mam and Dad-dad, but she obviously knew words like 'walk'.

'Oh, all right,' I said.

So I found Vanessa's coat and boots and gloves and woolly hat and after a great deal of struggling stuffed her into them. Then I strapped her into her push-chair and set off, hearing Aunt Patsy's promise that she would have tea ready on our return.

I had intended to fall into a romantic reverie—this was where the Land Rover had met me each morning when I was on the archaeological dig last summer; this was the road I had walked arm in arm with Alastair; this was the bridge where we used to kiss goodnight—but Vanessa made such a mood difficult if not impossible.

There she was, bundled up so that only her little flower-like face showed, waving her mittened paws, and gabbling away in her own incomprehensible language.

'I'm terribly unhappy,' I told her.

'Glug,' said Vanessa cheerfully.

'All men are beasts.'

'Coo.'

'They're fickle and boorish and insensitive.'

'Gluglug.'

'I'll never love anyone again.'

'Wah wah.'

'But I still love him,' I wailed, 'I still love him.'

Vanessa this time remained silent. But she gave me a broad beautiful smile, showing pink gums and two stumps of teeth like hazel kernels.

'Vanessa, you're gorgeous, I adore you.'

I bent to kiss her cold nose and gave up the conversation.

'Stop talking nonsense. Say "Emma", "Emma". I'm your cousin and you ought to know my name by now, "Emma".'

Vanessa smiled again and waved her arms up and down, like the conductor of an orchestra.

The track up to the dig was too muddy for the pushchair so, after about fifty yards, I gave up. I no longer wanted to go there. I no longer wanted to think about Alastair. It was absurd and sentimental to dwell on past kisses. And it would be even more absurd to day-dream about beguiling him in my black velvet dress.

The only way to regain my self-respect and peace of mind was to write him a cheerful, dignified letter, telling him that I thought we should stop seeing each other; that I would always remember our wonderful summer together; that absence might be all right for very solidly-based lovers but for people who had only just met, it didn't work.

It would not be a completely sincere letter, for one of the reasons for writing it was my inability to express my thoughts and feelings to Alastair without doubting his understanding them.

Perhaps in two or three years' time we would meet as equals at some archaeological conference and re-discover our love but I had no real confidence in such a prospect. In any case, it would then be a different sort of love. The sort I had been suffering from for the last six months was over. Or would be when I had written the letter.

'Dear Alastair, it just isn't working out, is it? You're involved in your life and I'm involved with mine and we don't seem to be able to bridge the gap. So I am writing to say goodbye ... for the present at any rate....' I began writing the letter in my head. I hoped I would be strong-minded enough to post it.

A sudden lifting of my spirits made me realise that my decision was the right one. I did not want to spend the rest of my life waiting for telephone calls and sobbing in diesel trains, avoiding friendships with other people, boring or worrying my family. I did not want to become one of those miserable characters in Victorian novels who had been 'disappointed in love' and were always referred to with the adjective 'poor'. 'Poor Emma', indeed.

I would go to concerts with John, and drink coffee with school friends, and go to parties, and take part in musical evenings at home with Richard, Pauline and Peter. And I would get to know Joe better and take some interest in Nigeria and other world problems.

How peaceful it would be not to be in love!

'Vanessa,' I said, 'I've been a fool. But you've cured me.' And I began to sing to her.

The sun had just slipped over the horizon, but if I hurried round the bend in the road, I would be in time to see the sunset, rose and golden clouds in an icy green sky, and gold streaks across the darkening sea.

In the cottage the fire would be blazing, the kettle on and, if Aunt Patsy had remembered, the table laid for tea—bread and our Christmas honeycomb. How hungry I felt.